W9-AUK-753

THE VISITORS

PATRICIA C. MCKISSACK

FREDRICK L. MCKISSACK

JOHN MCKISSACK

THE VISITORS

THE CYBORG ACT

- All cyborgs must be registered with the Bureau of Cyborg Affairs (BCA).

- Those that are cyborgs must live within designated areas set aside on the Moon Colony. If a cyborg desires to live or work elsewhere, it must acquire BCA permission.

- It is mandated that cyborgs may not serve as officers in the World Federation of Nations' defense forces, serve in any national law enforcement agencies, or hold public office.

- Cyborg children must attend one of four cyborg academies based on test scores and abilities.

- Imprinting the ability to mimic human emotions into a clone's behavioral patterns is forbidden.

- A clone that disobeys a direct order must immediately be taken to a processing center for decommissioning.

- Instructing a clone to lie is restricted.

- Since clones are not citizens, they may not participate in elections.

THE CLONE CODES

- All clones are to be identified by number or alphanumerical designation. The use of names is restricted.

- Clones have no rights under a court of law and are recognized solely as property.

- Groups of clones in excess of three are not permitted without direct human supervision.

- Attempting to educate a clone beyond its work model specifications is forbidden and punishable in accordance with article 3C74.

- The manufacture of a clone in the likeness of a child is a capital offense.

To Bliss Elyse . . . who has made our family complete in so many ways. P.C.M., F.L.M., J.M.

Library of Congress Cataloging-in Publication Data available

ISBN 978-0-439-92987-5

10 9 8 7 6 5 4 3 2 1   12 13 14 15 16

Printed in the United States of America   23

First edition, February 2012
Book design by Phil Falco

THE THIRD BOOK OF THE CLONE CODES

SCHOLASTIC PRESS
NEW YORK

- All cyborgs over the age of 16 must be employed.
- Cyborgs need permission from the BCA to marry or have children.
- The BCA will provide cyborgs with medical insurance and health-care needs.
- Cyborgs cannot inherit real property.
- Cyborgs can only participate in amateur or professional sports within the Cyborg Leagues.

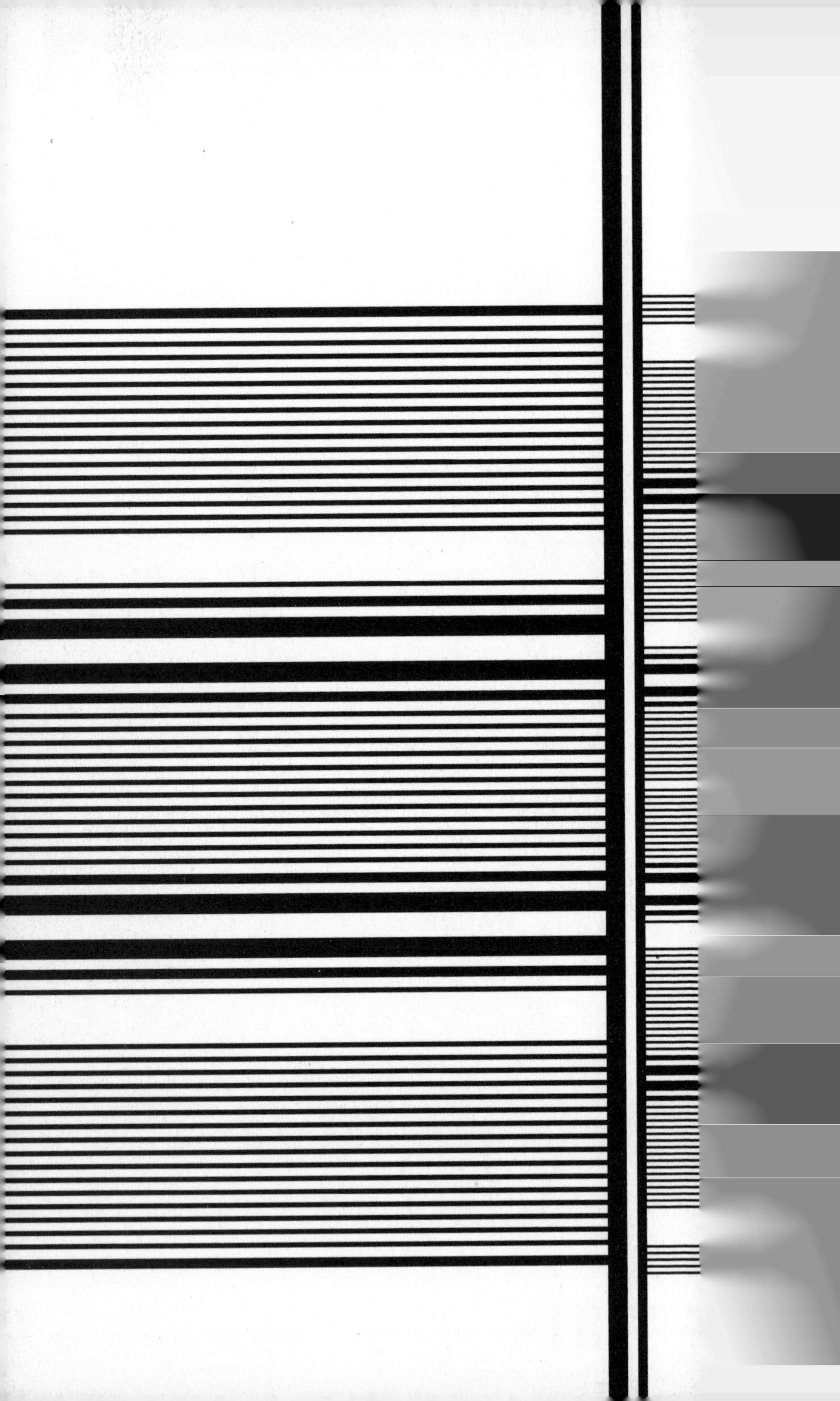

These are the beings that inhabit this universe:

FIRSTS

The highest order of human beings, Firsts, is a superior race. Firsts are all human. Firsts have the most advanced level of brain function — emotional capability and reasoning power. Firsts are smarter, cleaner, quicker, and more advanced than all other beings.

THE WHOLERS

The Wholers are a human supremacy group. The Wholer philosophy is that any human with even one artificial body part is not pure and therefore unacceptable. Wholer cells are first generation. Wholers consider themselves to be supreme beings — whole, pure, nothing synthetic. All Wholers are Firsts, but all Firsts are not Wholers. Under the recently passed Wholer Act, anyone with as little as one synthetic body part — but still considered a First — is now classified as a cyborg.

CLONES

Clones constitute the lowest order of humanoid. Clones have second-generation cells. They are inferior and are called Seconds. They are replicas of humans only in their physical makeup. Clones are not capable of feeling emotions. They cannot reason or think abstractly. Clones are owned by Firsts for the purpose of labor. Clones are living organisms patented by Topas Corporation International. Clones are governed by the laws of the Clone Codes, issued by the Clone Humane Society, the government agency for the protection and processing of clones.

THE YEAR IS 2171

Welcome.

I'm Carlos Pace, the son of Dr. Marcus Pace. I'm a gemaginist, a genius with a superior imagination.

I invite you to read the transcript of my memory stick, a computer program with personal data recorded. As you read, the words will give you a stream of visuals. Tied to them are the emotions and feelings attached to the events experienced by the subject. Before we begin, let me introduce you to those who have made this journey so memorable:

Dr. Marcus Pace is the director of the Federation's space program, and a member of the Wholers, an organization that believes in the superiority of human beings called Firsts.

Houston Ye, a cyborg pilot, is a college student.

Toby Ye is Houston's brother and past member of the Federation 22 special forces.

Leanna Deberry is an illegal clone who has grown up as a First. Now she is being hunted by the Federation.

Dr. Annette Deberry is Leanna's mom. She's the leader of The Liberty Bell Movement.

Dr. Anatol Ayala, Leanna's pediatrician and scientist, is a co-leader of The Liberty Bell Movement. He and Annette have been friends for many years.

Li Rizin, manager of the Moon mining colony, heads up the Moonborgs, cyborgs who live on the Moon.

Taylor Graham is the wicked, self-serving High Chancellor of the Federation.

Now that you know those who are part of this incredible universe, come laugh with me, learn with me. Experience my fear and my compassion. Let my pride swell your chest and my anger ball your fists. Come be inspired by the story of my friends and me as we continue the fight for freedom and justice for all.

Sincerely,

Carlos Pace

THE FIRST VISIT OF THE O

July 1787

In an upstairs, rented room on Market Street near Independence Hall, a weary Benjamin Franklin pulled on his nightshirt, said his prayers, and crawled into bed. He was about to blow out the bedside candle, when two sinister figures materialized at the foot of his bed. Obviously shaken, Franklin wiped his eyes and blinked. Then he mumbled something about the insufferable heat and the stress of drafting the Constitution wearing on his nerves. "Hallucination. That is all!"

"Don't doubt your sanity," the visitors answered in a reassuring way.

Mustering his courage, Franklin thrust the lamp into the darkened corner and called out, "Friend or foe? Devil or angel? By what magic did you enter my locked chamber?"

"We mean you no harm." The two beings melted into the shadows.

October 1896

"State the nature and intent of this intrusion!" Supreme Court Justice John Harlan placed his pen in the silver inkwell on his desk and nervously shoved his spectacles on his nose, adding, "Thievery, no doubt?" The black-hooded creatures that appeared in his Washington office looked ominous but they made no threatening moves. Harlan continued tentatively, "Take what you will, but I — I have no money!"

"We mean you no harm," said the mysterious specters.

January 1942

"You just can't walk into the White House private quarters. . . ." Mrs. Eleanor Roosevelt said, her voice shrill with emotion. She paused when she realized that the invaders had done just that — walked into the bedroom of the First Lady of the United States, straight through a solid wall.

"I guess you can," she whispered, more to herself than to anyone. Then pulling herself tall, she braced for what was to come, speaking with more confidence than she felt. "You must know there are guards right outside my door. All I need to do is scream out."

"We mean you no harm," said the strangers.

August 2047

"Did the corporations send you?" shouted David Montgomery. Although he wore the academic collar of a doctor, he was not a physician, but a young graduate student in medical research at Northwestern University. Fearlessly, Montgomery placed himself between the intruders and the prototype of his adult-cloning stabilizer. "Just because they're paying for my research doesn't mean they own my every thought. I am not selling my invention. Go tell them that!"

"We mean you no harm," said the strange life-forms. "We come in peace but with an important message. Earthlings have mastered the technology necessary for intergalactic space travel. Yet you will not be ready."

"Intergalactic travel!" exclaimed Franklin. "By what manner of witchcraft do you come by this knowledge? And why am I privileged or cursed to know it?"

"There is no sorcery involved. We experience time in a different way. We are speaking to many of you at the same time."

"I am expected to believe that you traveled here from the stars?" Justice Harlan said, shaking his head, unable to go on.

"You can see our future! How is this possible?" said Roosevelt, taking a seat at a small Victorian desk. She took out a tablet and pen. "Do you mind if I take notes? Please go on."

"We are with Justice Harlan in 1896, but we are also in 1787 with Benjamin Franklin, 1942 with Eleanor Roosevelt, 2047 with David Montgomery, and a young girl in 2170."

"All at the same time?" Roosevelt scribbled in her notebook.

"There are countless pasts, presents, and futures, all recorded on grids, like ribbons that stretch into infinity. As decisions are made and problems solved along the grids, outcomes are altered and events change."

"Spherical time!" shouted Montgomery. "One of my professors studied the whirlpool theory for years. He would have died a happy man if he'd known about you. What are you called?" he added.

"You may call us The O."

"So the old myths are true," whispered Montgomery. "The O do exist."

Franklin thrust the candle into the darkness once more to get a better look at his visitors. The O retreated. Franklin shrugged. "We are still a sovereign nation in 2170?"

The aliens explained further. "Unless you change your ways, you will be stopped at the threshold of space."

"Change in what way?" Montgomery asked.

"You must keep liberty alive!" the aliens answered.

"We are struggling to stay free now," said Franklin.

"We are fighting tyranny on the battlefield as we speak," said Mrs. Roosevelt.

"Our world is a far better place than it was a hundred years ago," said Montgomery. "We haven't had a war in over fifty years. Nations have worked together to conquer many diseases so people are living longer and better in safer and healthier environments. Surely, we should get points for that."

"We do not tolerate oppression of any sentient beings beyond your borders. For us, liberty and justice for all is not a motto but a reality," said The O.

Roosevelt was obviously upset. "What are you talking about? Your ultimatum seems to come straight from Hollywood or a very bad science fiction novel. We humans do value freedom, justice, and peace. We're capable of making decisions and solving our own problems without your interference."

"We were sent to deliver a message: *They are not rocks.* Consider yourself warned."

"*They are not rocks?* What does that mean?" asked Justice Harlan.

"It will be made clear," the visitors said.

"What will you do if we come out in space, anyway?" Montgomery insisted.

"Just remember: They are not rocks." The visitors vanished.

THE MAKING
FEAR

MEMORY STICK
SECTOR F-2
THE MAKING

"I don't know why I'm doing this," I mumble to myself. "But I just have to know what Leanna went through during her Making at the Topas Corporation." I close my eyes and relax. "One deep breath, two deep breaths," I continue whispering.

I can't concentrate through the swirling fog that fills my thoughts. I've lost my name somewhere in the haze. Without a name, who are you? Who am I?

I strain to find the letters, one by one. Yes. C-A-R-L-O-S. My name is Carlos — Carlos Pace. I hold on to the name like it's a lifeline. I'm ten years old. My parents are Dr. Marcus Pace, an astro-engineer, and Dr. Penelope Pace, a biophysicist.

Suddenly, I remember riding the waves at the water park last summer. The water is warm. Rolling waves toss me about. I play all day. The memory of my house is fading. Darkness comes, pushing out the loving feeling I have of my mother humming me to sleep in my bed made up with Marvo Man sheets.

Where am I now? It's so hard for me to concentrate. S-s-sleepy. I fall, fall, fall into the arms of dread — the Making.

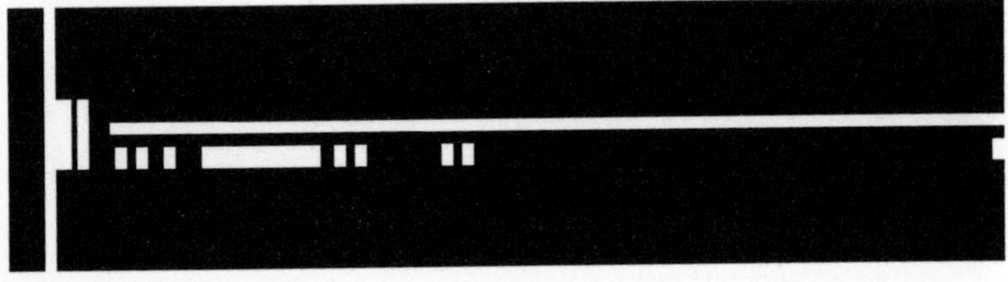

MEMORY STICK
SECTOR F-3
LEANNA'S EXPERIENCE

"Carlos. Carlos, are you all right?" I am breathless and wet with panic and pain. "Carlos! Stop screaming. Tell me what's wrong!" Leanna's voice yanks me out of the dark place where I had been taken by her memory stick. I've decided that was a silly thing to do. I know for sure.

It all began after we rescued Houston and Toby from the chancellor's office. Great movie action. We were hiding out, like the Dalton Gang of nineteenth-century America. The chancellor of the Federation even had a bounty for each of us. Frisk!

For a while, we used the ship's camouflage system, blending in with the surroundings. But there's a limit on how long RUBy can hold the ship in chameleon mode, so we moved to Mount Everest to wait for things to die down. Rizin was sure no one would look for us there. He turned out to be right.

When Rizin felt it was time, we made our way to Cyborg City hovering over Omaha, Nebraska. Our ship is docked on the giant hover barge filled with junk and throw-away stuff from everywhere on the Earth. The floating junkyard, like its sister barge, known as Gypsy City, provides fuel and hard-to-find parts for just about anything.

Rizin called for Epps, Houston, and several other cyborgs to join him in tactical plans. It's hard to keep count of the times Rizin has stated our objectives. "First, we are committed to keeping Leanna free until she is granted an open trial. Her existence will prove that clones are independent beings and should be free. The second goal is equally as important," Rizin always adds. "We want civil rights for the cyborgs. No more second-class citizenship." Then raising his fist in victory, Rizin ends with a cry for action. "Justice!"

"Justice!" we always respond.

Before leaving the ship, Dr. Epps pulled me to the side. "Leanna's resting. I've cleared her mind of the horrible ordeal she experienced at the Topas Corporation and placed them in a memory stick," Epps explained in her military officer's voice.

Epps had a brilliant medical career in the air guard. Then she crashed in an out-of-the-way place somewhere in New Zealand. The surgeons gave her six artificial parts. Saved her life, but ended her career. Epps is a certified cyborg, and no less a superior doctor, but her practice is limited to the Moon Colony, far removed from the medical establishment. No more awards and recognition, just the appreciation of her fellow cyborgs.

"We'll treat Leanna's artificial purple skin, and she'll be back to her normal self after a few more treatments." Then Epps gave me the cylinder for safekeeping, saying, "Give it to her when she awakes."

As soon as Epps left, Houston approached me. I was wondering what he was going to tease me about this time.

But I could see he wasn't in a playful mood. "I know this is asking a lot," Houston said, "but may I take RUBy to the meeting? She could be so helpful with our plans."

"It's not my approval you need. Ask RUBy."

"What?" Houston had a frown on his face. All I could think about was, *I've done it again . . . made Houston suspicious.*

"Ask RUBy? Ask a computer?"

I was looking for a quick way out. . . . The memory stick in my hand. No hard decision for me. I was thinking just then, it would be so jazz if I experienced Leanna's Making. If RUBy went with Houston, then she wouldn't be around to talk me out of snooping in Leanna's memories.

Houston was pleased.

Now I wish RUBy had been with me. I am still out of it, fighting my way back.

"Carlos, come on, can you hear me?" Leanna is calling.

Leanna's face is twisted with confusion and concern. She pulls me up from the cold metal floor of the crew lounge. "You were screaming like a banshee, flaying about in terror. What in the name of Aunt Betsy have you been doing?"

I gather my thoughts before answering. With no more pain, and no more fear, I am able to handle the overwhelming emotions. "Do you remember anything about what happened to you at the Topas Corporation down in Argentina? You know, when they tried to alter you into a clone?" I ask sheepishly.

Leanna looks at me with a hint of suspicion. "Hey, look! I've got purple skin and it doesn't wash off, so yes, I remember that awful place that manufactures people. Epps zapped the memories of the Making process and packed them in a memory stick."

"Why did Epps want you to have the memories?" I say, not really wanting to know the answer.

"Epps thinks the information might help find a way to deprogram other clones —" Leanna stops mid-sentence. "Carlos. Did you open it?" Leanna is clearly upset.

I try to explain. "I'm making a memory stick of my own adventures. One day I will share it with people who think clones are stupid and cyborgs are brutes. Like my dad. He's a Wholer who believes Firsts are superior to everybody."

"What's that got to do with my memories?" Leanna doesn't believe a thimbleful of what I've said. I can feel the heat of her anger spiraling.

I decide to stop the game playing and out the truth. "Epps told me to give you the stick but wait until you woke."

"Okay. Keep going. . . ."

"I waited. I waited and thought I'd get a better idea of how it feels to be a clone by experiencing what you went through. Don't be mad. Please."

"Carlos!"

I can hear it in Leanna's voice. She's ready to give me a smack, but not a beat down. She throws a pretend punch, tapping my nose, then she shakes her head.

"Forgive me," I plead, on bended knee.

"Never!"

I slide to the floor and rest my head against the back of the chair and stretch my legs out. Leanna joins me. "Hey, Wonderboy," she says, closing her eyes as she leans back her head. "One of these days, your curiosity will get you gobbled up by the wolf." She punches me, then flashes a half smile. "The funny thing is," she adds, "the wolf would spit you out, because you're full of crap."

We laugh. Then we are quiet. I imagine *comfortable* is a word for what it feels like being wrapped in a well-used quilt.

The dark circles under Leanna's eyes show that she's suffered a lot. Yet, she seems curious about my experience. "The way you were screaming, Carlos, it must have been scary," she says. "I don't remember a thing about the Making. Still, I know I don't want to experience it again — later for research, maybe, but not right now."

"Don't even think about opening that stick," I jump in.

"That bad, huh?"

"Want me to tell you about it?" I ask.

"I think not. . . ." Leanna answers, sounding uncertain. She pulls her knees up and folds her arms around them.

I answer the unasked question. "Telling about the Making is different than experiencing the strong memories with all the emotions attached."

"Okay, then, I guess . . . sure."

MEMORY STICK
SECTOR F-4
TELLING

The water is warm like waves in a water park. Rolling waves toss me as I play.

I feel sleepy in this pitch-black darkness. I'm floating in something thick and gooey. The stuff is very sweet as it touches my tongue and fills the inside of my nose. It's sweeter than syrup. Too sweet. I try to spit it out, but the taste won't go away.

It's hard to breathe as my mouth fills with more and more syrupy stuff. The inside of my nose starts to burn. Two tubes have been pushed up in them so that I can breathe among all this gooeyness.

I try to stay calm, but I'm gagging. I keep my mouth shut, not wanting to swallow the warm syrup.

How long have I been here?

I'm so tired. Did I fall asleep again?

Oh, do my eyes hurt. The bright lights stab at me. It's worse than someone poking my eyes with a stick. I can't move my arms and legs in all this thickness.

I can't move my hands, either. They've been tied with ropes.

I'm stuck in some kind of glass jar, with wires connected to my body.

I start to cry, and soon sleep takes over.

When I wake, I'm choking, gagging even harder. And I'm shivering.

The syrup is gone. But now I'm in salty water. A tube pushes icy liquid into my throat.

My body knows to swallow. My stomach fills quickly.

There are no more wires, just the tubes in my mouth and nose.

When I glance at my hands, I see they are bright orange. My *whole body* is orange.

There are voices in my head now, talking loudly.

This clone is #9577

This clone wants to work.

This clone is happy.

This clone is #9577.

This clone wants to work.

This clone is happy.

This clone is #9577.

This clone wants to work.

This clone is happy.

"Stop!" I scream.

A gulp of salty water rushes down my throat. I gag.

My mind races; I need to get out of here. Can I bust the glass body tube I'm in? My hands bounce off the unbreakable glass. Pounding harder and harder. My fear feels like an inflating balloon inside my chest, same as the time I locked myself in the hall closet — no way out, pure panic.

Just when I feel like I'm going over a waterfall, the bottom to my watery prison opens and all the salt water rushes out, threatening to take me with it. Instead, I am held up by a big, burly man wearing a midnight blue shirt and pants. My eyes are fixed on his shirt pocket with red letters: CLONE HUMANE SOCIETY MAKER.

He slams me down on a cold metal table. Naked and chilled, I try to stop shivering. The lights above hurt my eyes.

"Who are you?" the man asks.

"I think my name is . . . I can't find my name."

The man slaps me across my face. I'm filled with fear.

"You're clone number 9577! Say it! *I am clone number 9577.*"

I'm completely orange and confused. I fight not to lose control — control of what? I am me, but I am not me. I don't even know who me is. I feel lost, lost in a dark forest with crazy things lurking around. Still, I won't say that I'm a clone. "I am not a clone," I dare to say. "Never!"

The back of the Maker's hand whacks me on the side of my head, knocking me facedown to the floor.

I thought it was bad, but each time I resisted, the beatings got stronger. A bamboo stick slashes across my bare back. I beg the Maker for mercy. He laughs. I vomit.

"Clone!"

"I'm still not a clone. My name is . . ." I struggle hard, pushing my brain to the limit to just find my name. "Carlos . . . Carlos Pace." There is some of me left. There is some Leanna left.

"Carlos, enough!" Leanna shouts. "Don't tell me any more. No more, please."

I am physically shaking — from the cold and from what I've

been through. "I don't care what my dad believes," I mumble, struggling to stand up. "I had no idea of what clones truly go through in the Making process. Leanna, you really suffered. But you resisted. You never gave in. I am so proud to be your friend. If I had a sister, I'd want her to be just like you."

"And I wouldn't mind having a real genius little brother like you, too," Leanna says, laughing.

"Am I forgiven for opening your memory stick?"

"NO!"

Leanna leads me to a more comfortable lounge chair. Her eyes become serious. "Carlos, Epps wiped the incident out of my mind, and frankly, after having you describe it, I feel she was right."

"I think so, too."

"That's it. . . . You need to do more *thinking*." Leanna crosses her arms. I feel her getting upset again. "Next time, *think* before acting. *Do dumb, get dumb results,* my mom always says. I shouldn't have to tell an award-winning math and science prodigy with a fantastic imagination — a *gemaginist* — to think!"

"I hear you," I say, wishing Leanna and Houston hadn't found out that I was inducted into the Steven Jobs International Gemaginists League a month before we met. It would have been a secret forever if I had to tell, but I was outed by the People's Network.

"You should let Epps give you a look," Leanna is saying, "just to make sure there's not any psychological damage that might show up later."

Leanna's right about the thinking part. Suppose she had gone with the others to Cyborg City, and I'd been left alone? I might have been driven mad by the intensity of the experience.

"Hey, I'm okay." I decide not to upset her any more.

Leanna rubs her purple, bald head, a bitter reminder of her Topas nightmare. "I hope my hair grows back sooner rather than later." No matter what they try to do to Leanna, they can't make her a clone — not the kind they Make at the Topas Corporation.

"Carlos and Leanna," Rizin's voice interrupts our conversation. "To the bridge, now."

"Oh, by the way," Leanna says, tapping me on the back of my head. "You're forgiven."

If I could light my thoughts like RUBy, I'd be a loud orange with hints of green — happy and fresh.

CYBORG CITY
LIBERTY

MEMORY STICK
SECTOR F-6
CYBORG CITY

Cyborg City is the unofficial headquarters for the freedom protests — a Federation target. Cyborgs, along with The Liberty Bell, have been protesting against the inhumane treatment of clones and the second-class citizenship of cyborgs over the past three months. The Federation is holding firm against it, though some countries are beginning to argue for changes to be made in order to keep the peace.

"Cowards," yells Rizin. "They claim to want to do the right thing, but for all the wrong reasons."

"It's about what the Topas Corporation wants that matters," says Leanna.

"Who cares, as long as we get what we want," argues Houston.

"Peace can never stand without truth as its foundation," says Rizin, quoting Santos Rodgers, the first chancellor of The World Federation of Nations (The WFN). He was an exceptional leader and an honorable man. Heads are nodding all around.

Rizin is dead center.

I wish Dad could hear this. He would be surprised at Rizin's moderate reasoning. Dad is double wrong when it comes to cyborgs, beginning with his definition of them.

"Cyborgs are monsters," I've heard Dad say a hundred times. But it isn't true. I've learned a lot being with Houston and all the other cyborgs on this adventure. I understand that cyborgs have biofe external parts, and they may look a little strange, but they aren't monsters. Cyborgs are not unfortunates who know nothing but violence.

I'm a kid and I know better; still, it's hard for some people, especially extremists like the Wholers who don't want to know the truth.

"Never let your guard down. Always remember they are cyborgs," Dad preached constantly.

Yet, I owe my life to cyborg Houston Ye, the best friend a person can have.

Naturally, Rizin can be terrifying at first. Truth is, when he gets in a rage, he's still scary. Rizin's biofe eyes always seem to be moving, probing, bouncing from one thing to another, searching for an enemy who might be hiding in a food canister. And his gnarled and twisted hands with missing fingers are tattooed with the C-within-a-circle cyborg mark.

What gets me is the tattoo of a black king cobra with green eyes that encircles Rizin's shoulder and back. I shiver every time I see the thing. It's his *Familiar.*

Every cyborg gets one when he comes of age. Imagine touching Rizin's tattoo or one of a tiger, snake, wolf, bear, or whatever you choose, and it leaps to life as your fighting partner? Talk about frisk! I'd love to have a jaguar as my companion warrior. I can't help but laugh. Wouldn't Dad have a fall-down fit if I got a tattoo that could leap to life? A Familiar? Not that any cyborg would let me have one. But I like to imagine it, anyway.

Rizin speaks to Leanna and me. "The chancellor knows everything now from Houston's mind-drain. But we've been warned by one of our fake First infiltrators that the chancellor is sending ships to destroy Cyborg City."

Rizin sighs. He flexes his muscles, then grabs Leanna and me by our shoulders and pulls us to him. "You two should be playing games, swifting and having fun, not fighting battles. . . ." His voice trails off. He releases us. I admit, his move was scary at first, but I quickly realize that Rizin cares — deeply cares. It's hard to get rid of ideas no matter how hard I try.

Rizin turns off the handheld commpad, to which he'd connected RUBy during the planning session on the Moon. Meanwhile, he shares what's been happening. "The chancellor has sent his biobots," he says angrily. "Killer robots!"

"We must stop him," I immediately put in. "Protect Leanna."

"Right," Rizin says, then he goes on to explain. "Graham will never give us a fair fight. So, we're going to torch the city ourselves."

In his mind, this city is the holding ground for his enemies. But, if the city blows, we build another one. If the three hundred people inside are destroyed, our movement will be severely crippled. "We've got to get the people off. Not too much time to do it, either."

"We won't let him," I say strongly, with clenched teeth and balled fists.

Rizin gives me a quick glance. "I like your spirit, kid."

Wow . . . Rizin says he likes my spirit. I didn't know he knew I was alive. I think I get on his nerves. Maybe . . . But right now, I feel like a real team member.

Panic.

Looking out the window, I spot Houston and Tools in a fierce hand-to-foot battle with biobots, the flesh-eating robots!

From the safety of our ship, we have a panoramic view of the city's deck. Biobots are leaping off hovercraft with their accordion legs attached to a giant ball with tentacles waving around like an octopus.

I stumble backward with a gasp when a biobot is slammed against our ship's front window. I get a good look at its mouth with four rows of metal teeth, and I am reminded that these creatures are vicious, skilled fighters that eat the flesh of their victims — human flesh.

Houston taps the tattoo on the side of his neck and his Familiar, a wolf named Apache, leaps to life and joins Houston in the fight. It's a terrifying sight.

Rizin touches the command keys ordering the ship's computer to stand ready.

"Hi, I'm back," chirps RUBy's young girl's voice. "So glad to be with you again."

I'm glad to see her, too, but I'm going to have fun with her, tease a little. "So what do you care about being here with me?" I say, sounding gruff. "You were so anxious to leave, just ran off with the first person who offered you a ride!"

Rizin raises his head. "Now that's a first." He throws up his arms. "Boy genius jealous of computer girlfriend."

Busted.

I look right at Leanna. "I didn't mean it like that. . . ." Her eyes are laughing.

"Don't you dare say one word," I grumble. "Or else!'

"I don't get it," says RUBy. "What?"

"It's best you don't get it," Leanna says, dismissing my threat.

I walk over to the window. "I didn't mean it to sound like girlfriendy stuff . . . you know?"

"Yeah, we know," Rizin puts in just before he goes out to join the fight. There's the hint of a smile on his face. I'm so embarrassed. I look out the window. It's strange. My friends are in a fight to the death and I'm joking about girlfriend stuff. None of this seems real.

The whole scene looks like an old-fashioned video game: *Shoot anything that moves.*

Apache leaps in the air, crashing into the flesh-eating monster creeping up behind Houston. The biobot slides across the deck, stopping in front of our window. Before it can get up, Rizin hacks off its head. Cyborgs inside the city are holding the biobots off with blasters. One by one the flesh eaters die or fall back.

"Sorry, your dinner plans have been changed," we hear Rizin shout to the biobots.

Houston kicks an attacker's legs, and as it stumbles around on twisted legs, it becomes an easy kill for Apache.

A ship's horn blows and the biobots retreat.

"Run, run," Leanna shouts to Houston, as the attackers flee. "We need to get out of here before more of them show up."

Rizin barks orders as he returns to the bridge. He opens the large cargo doors, then turns to me.

"Carlos, program RUBy to lift off with a course set for the Moon . . . when I give the command." Rizin points to a huge crowd of people running toward the ship. "We have to be off Cyborg City in fifteen minutes. The timer is activated. The place is set to blow. Got it?"

"Yes, sir," I answer, more confident than I'm feeling.

"Good. You're doing your father proud," he says, not knowing my dad would be a mental case if he saw me taking orders from a renegade cyborg. . . . How would Dad say it? — *Consorting with enemies of the state.*

Rizin hurries his instructions. "I'm heading back to help Houston, Epps, and Tools with the evacuation. Again, we only have a few minutes, so stay alert," Rizin says, and quickly leaves the bridge.

"Don't mess up," Leanna says, never taking her eyes off the spectacle outside.

"Rizin has personally asked me to do this," I say. "That makes it special, so I won't mess up."

I like being scared and excited at the same time. My heart speeds up and my body moves faster. Scientifically, I know they're caused by a blast of adrenaline. But I think of the feeling as a zest rush — an all-natural, gusto high.

"RUBy, are you ready?" I ask, my voice filled with excitement.

"How is a girlfriend supposed to answer?" RUBy asks, wanting to get it right.

I jump back as if stung by a jellyfish. "Girlfriend? Girlfriend!" I shout. I had to stop this craziness once and for all. "You are not my girlfriend. You are . . . are a rock!"

The moment I say it, I want to take it back, but misspoken words are like a torn feather pillow. Once spoken, words are like flying feathers. They can't be retrieved.

"Sorry, I didn't mean . . ."

RUBy gasps and goes silent. The screen goes dark, not a flicker of a light.

"Carlos, how could you be so cruel?" Leanna won't look at me.

How can I be so responsible one minute, only to feel like a dead fish in the next few seconds? I don't know, but here I am. Leanna leaves the bridge in a huff and RUBy remains quiet.

Meanwhile, cyborgs of all shapes and sizes are running to the ship. Some have no special external enhancements, just like Houston. They could pass for Firsts, but that's why cyborgs are required to wear tattoos. Removal of a cyborg tattoo is an international offense that could land them on the Mars penal colony.

Many of the other cyborgs running toward the ship are stereotypes of what Firsts use to scare little children — an assortment of artificial parts placed in strange places. A good example is Tools, who has four arms with laser blasters extended from each hand. I was frightened of him when we met, but now I truly enjoy his offbeat humor and silly smile. So what if Tool's partner, Stick, has a mouth in his palm. I enjoy him, too.

And Epps is a medical doctor who can take out a biobot in two moves. She just went back to help a group get out of the city and make it to the ship. Seconds tick away. Epps can't make it. . . .

"There is a Federation warship approaching," RUBy announces flatly. "We have twenty seconds before we are programmed to leave."

"We're not going to reach the ship," Epps calls in on her commglasses.

"Sorry, Epps," Rizin responds. Then to his crew, he snaps the order, "Close the doors."

To my horror, there are about sixty people running with Epps, just seconds away from the cargo doors.

"Rizin," I call, "we can't leave or all those people will die, especially Epps. She's a friend and you don't treat friends like that."

"We will be blasting off in ten seconds," says Rizin. "We are cyborgs and we all know the risks. Close the door! . . . What do you mean, the door won't close?" Rizin yells. "RUBy, Carlos, what are you doing? Let the doors close!"

"It's not me," I call.

Meanwhile, the remaining escapees dash for the doors that are still open. At the same time, a laser beam shoots over our bow and blasts into Cyborg City. A cascade of preset explosives begin exploding, engulfing the floating city in flames. Time is out!

RUBy returns fire, knocking out the attacker's wing stabilizer — a minor inconvenience. The Federation ship flees to safety on the ground to reset, so it can return to the fight.

"Everybody's on board. Can we go now?" Rizin says in a fury.

The exterior doors slam, and RUBy soars out of orbit. Behind us, Cyborg City explodes in a fireball.

"You saved all those people, RUBy. You're a treasure."

Truth is, if I ever wanted a girlfriend, I'd want her to be just as smart, kind, and brave as RUBy.

"Thanks, friend," I whisper.

Still no answer.

I should have known she wouldn't answer me right away. Oh, well, I'll keep doing whatever's needed to get my friend back.

MOON BASE
ANXIETY

MEMORY STICK
SECTOR L-2
SHACKLETON

We've reached the Moon mining base, a biosphere. The Federation has a Moon base governor everybody affectionately calls Big House. Rizin is the highest-ranking Federation base manager. Everybody knows he runs the place.

We've made it to the base long before the Federation ships will reach Shackleton, so Rizin's people have disembarked and made their way down to the domed city. There, they will be cared for, fed, and given quarters until it is decided what the next step will be.

Houston, his brother Toby, and Rizin have gone to the base to make plans to defend the Moon when the Federation attack forces arrive and how to hold and defend Leanna until she gets her day in court. Meanwhile, that allows me some free time.

When I was here before, I found out the base was named after the massive moon crater in which the domed city is built, Shackleton. The crater is named after the nineteenth-century explorer Sir Ernest Shackleton. His band of adventurers was stranded in the frozen Antarctica for nearly two years with no chance for a rescue. Like the Shackleton crew of 1914, the Moonborgs are experts at survival, too.

Big House was a First until the Wholer Act was passed, making anybody with one artificial part a cyborg. The WFN Moon Operations Committee kept Big House on as the official governor of Shackleton, but not Rizin. He was removed from his duties, so the miners boycotted and refused to work, unless Rizin was hired back. So the committee did. But this time, I don't think the Federation will hire him again.

Here, clones, cyborgs, and Firsts are totally integrated. And it works. Nothing like the chaos the Wholers say would happen if clones and cyborgs were free on Earth.

Rizin's informant, the one who warned him about the attack on Cyborg City, also told him the chancellor has ordered a blockade of the Moon — to starve the Moonborgs into surrender. "This war plan has been used to capture cities for hundreds of years," says Leanna. "The chancellor is probably thinking, once the city runs out of food the citizens will give up without a fight," she explains.

I put in, "I don't think Chancellor Graham really knows cyborgs."

Rizin, Houston, and Toby return within the hour. Rizin always looks serious, but his expression is filled with . . . I'm feeling the word *dread.*

"It's been decided," he says. "I'm going to take twenty men to Mars. They will command the new Federation ships that are standing ready. With those ships, we can put some serious whup on The WFN tin buckets."

"What will you use to power them?" I ask, feeling very uneasy.

"I don't know yet." Rizins smirks. "Besides, I have RUBy and Carlos with me. Ain't but one ship, but what a great ship!"

Oh, no, what is Rizin planning? Does he want to use RUBy to go to war? She won't do it! I decide not to confront Rizin. RUBy can show her own feelings.

Rizin goes back to the base to choose the men who will accompany us to Mars and man the ships. After he returns, he says, "Come with me, Toby. We will need your help for sure. Sooner or later, the space marines will attack. We've got to be ready to hit them hard and fast. Those ships will do it for us."

"Are you all right with that, Toby?" Houston asks his brother while gulping down a grape slush-bob.

The brothers have just reunited after years of being separated by deceit and trickery. Chancellor Graham handpicked Toby to be the future commander of The WFN Special Forces. But when Toby learned the truth, Graham turned his back on him and dismissed him from active duty.

"Rizin, sir," Toby speaks directly. "I've trained all my life to be a good soldier and to protect and defend our planet from all foreign and domestic harm. Now we are preparing to steal WFN ships, consort with criminals, and attack Earth. I have no use for Chancellor Graham, but I still feel an allegiance to Earth and the people who live there."

"Did you know I was a Special Forces Federation officer?" Rizin says, standing nose to nose with Toby. "I understand your feelings. Loyalty. We're reading the same book. We need to get on the same page.

"Fix me one of those juice things," Rizin calls to Houston, who busily prepares Rizin a banana slush-bob. "Sprinkle a dab of chocolate and some nuts on top." Rizin licks his fingers as the chocolate runs down the cup.

All of us are quiet and still, trying not to call attention to ourselves.

"Toby, our goal is not to take over the Earth, or to hurt anyone there. We are trying to protect Leanna until we can get The WFN Supreme Court to set a date for her and The Liberty Bell court case. Leanna is not your typical clone."

Leanna picks it up from there. "We clones are not mindless lumps of flesh. I was allowed to grow from infancy and learn. We are no different from a First . . . or any other sentient beings."

"I — I thought clones were developed to serve their owners better, to be obedient servants," Toby says.

"Leanna is proof positive. It isn't a theory," Houston adds.

Rizin takes a gulp of his slush-bob. "Graham doesn't want that trial to take place, so to divert attention from the real issue, he has turned all those involved with the freedom movement into traitors and assassins."

"Yes. But. Should we trust the Mars prisoners? It is a penal colony," Toby asks.

Toby's a First, with all of the prejudices Firsts have about cyborgs and clones. His negative thoughts feel thick. I can cut them with a butter knife.

Leanna tells us to link our commglasses. "I think I can help Toby understand the importance of our mission."

MEMORY STICK
SECTOR G-9
THE ORIGINAL CUSTODIANS

Commglasses resemble an ordinary pair of sunglasses until I put them on. Instantly, I step into another world — able to go anywhere, see anything. My favorite hangout place is the joke factory. I can enjoy the funniest jokes and even play a prank on my friends. But not now.

Our commglasses connect with Leanna's, so that we all see and hear her program.

Our metal world on the lounge deck is replaced with Dr. Ayala's library back on Earth. The room is traditional with old-fashioned bookshelves filled with books of all sizes, leather chairs, and of course Dr. Ayala's desk. His office even smells old to me. "I grew up in this library," Leanna says.

The Liberty Bell Movement's other original custodians materialize in the room.

Mrs. Eleanor Roosevelt, upon seeing us, gleefully gives each of us a big hug. She looks like my grandmother, with her white pearl necklace and a silk print blouse that is scented with carnation flowers.

Leanna's great-grandfather, Dr. David Montgomery, bear-hugs Leanna. Holding her close, he extends his hand for

Houston to slap. I haven't seen anyone do that except in old, old movies. Dr. Montgomery then ruffles my black, curly hair, making it look messier than usual.

Benjamin Franklin politely bows, as a gentleman did in his day and time. Dressed plainly as always in his vest, coat, and necktie, he nods in turn to each of us.

"Welcome." United States Supreme Court Justice John Harlan gestures for all of us to sit down.

"It's been a while since I've seen you, Leanna. You're purple now," Dr. Montgomery begins.

Leanna notices Toby. He is moving around the room in amazement. "Program pause," she says.

Toby examines the room and the four custodians. "Fascinating. These aren't holograms. This is advanced tech? What?"

"These are holographs," Leanna explains. "Dr. Ayala developed the program just for me. They are my companions, replicas of the original custodians. Notice this." Leanna holds the hand of her great-grandfather. "Unlike a hologram that can't be touched, a holograph is solid in our world. I can hold Pap-Pap's hand."

Toby looks at Houston. "Well, little brother, this is impressive that you know people who can develop such things."

"No, we're not throwaways as you've been taught," Houston counters.

Toby lowers his eyes. I understand why, 'cause I've had some of those same bigoted thoughts. But I'm happy to be past that point. Toby is working on his prejudices, but it's hard to unlearn a belief.

Leanna tells the custodians what is happening. "Let me give you the short version. Mom and Dr. Ayala are back in prison, awaiting the treason trial. Chancellor Graham tried to make me an altered clone so The Liberty Bell Movement couldn't use me as evidence, but my friends rescued me. I'm all that's left of The Movement for clone liberation!" Leanna spews it out in one breath.

"The chancellor will try to stop the trial from ever happening," Justice Harlan says.

"But the chancellor must use *words*, not weapons to fight," Roosevelt says, squeezing Leanna's hands in a delightful show of joy.

"Well, how do we do this?" Houston asks.

"It's simple — show up in court with a wonderful lawyer. It's just that simple," Harlan answers with a smile. "If I had to choose a good lawyer for you, Leanna," he says, "I would get John Quincy Adams. He is the only lawyer to argue and win a slavery case before the United States Supreme Court. He would be your best chance. But . . ."

Interrupting Harlan, Toby says, "Computers can't be lawyers; only people can."

"Who knows what is possible?" Franklin says.

"This is all nice, but who are The O? And where do they fit in?" Toby asks.

"Well, when I first met you, way back when, The O appeared to me as I was looking at the glowing rocks in Dr. Pace's laboratory at Atlantis. The O came and said I was one of those in the first contact, with the message, *They are not rocks*."

"What did The O mean by that?" Toby asks.

"We have a few ideas, but we aren't sure," I say, careful not to reveal too much.

"I think I've seen enough for me to stick around," says Toby.

Rizin orders Toby to help Big House get ready for the invasion instead of going to Mars. "They need your leadership and training," Rizin tells Toby. "You will have nothing to be ashamed of. I hope you believe that."

"I wouldn't be going if I didn't believe it." Toby salutes Rizin, who salutes him back.

Toby and Houston embrace. "You're already a hero," Houston says, adding, "You don't have to prove a thing."

"I promise you this," I say to Toby. "RUBy won't do anything to hurt the Earth in any way."

End program.

RUBy has been silent, except for answering commands, since I called her a rock. Suddenly, her screen turns blazing white, then an arrow of blue light zooms into space. I've seen her do this several times before, but she's never told me what it's for.

"What did you just do?" Rizin asks RUBy.

She answers softly, "I contacted those who care."

"Where?" Leanna steps up.

"Mars," RUBy responds.

MEMORY STICK
SECTOR H-6
CARLOS AND RUBY

"Anybody in for a swifting match?" Leanna asks.

"Are you ready for a cyber-drop?" Houston responds playfully.

"Be careful with your jazz," I tease. "Leanna is tough."

The two of them leave the bridge, noisy and playful. I am with RUBy. Quiet. Alone.

The silence is as loud as a siren. I tighten my lips and swallow hard.

"The last few months have been intense." Yes! That's the right word — *intense.*

I'm a month away from being eleven years old, and right now, I miss my mom . . . and dad. Mom is as steady as sunrise. But Dad . . . I don't agree with him most of the time.

I transfer RUBy to my computer tablet, and we walk to the ship's observation star deck, a small room neatly tucked in the rear of the main engine deck.

I sit on a round bench, so that I can get a 360-degree view. I'm not sure about anyone else, but space makes me feel small and unimportant — like a falling leaf in a forest. Yet there is nothing brighter than the stars that spangle the darkness. It reminds me of black velvet with diamonds scattered here and there. Beautiful.

I love sitting here and chatting with my buddy. We come here often to share. I'm hoping RUBy will forgive me. I have to keep trying.

"RUBy," I begin the way I always do. "Have you ever heard the old myth about an evil Titan named Solar? He lives on the Sun where he defies any mortal to look upon his face. If you dare look, Solar will steal your eyesight." I hope RUBy answers.

"That's why on the Moon you should never look directly at the Earth's Sun without shields," she says, talking to me. Finally!

"RUBy you talked — to me — you're here?" I sputter, rushing ahead now that I have her attention. "Look, I'm sorry for calling you a rock! I didn't mean it."

"Harsh words are *brunt*, an ugly color that attacks my energy. Calling me a rock was brunt, but that's not why I haven't been talking very much. I'm about to make a transition, and I need to conserve my energy."

RUBy has never sounded so serious. Her bright colors bounce off the clear dome, making the room glow. "When you called me a rock," she says, "I realized that as close as we are, there is so little we really know about each other and our worlds."

"I know, and I'm sorry, multiplied by ten, for being an insensitive goof-goose," I add.

Without warning, two beings appear in the room. I know who they are instantly. They are dressed in dark, robelike garments, but where their faces are supposed to be, there are only flashing colors. RUBy responds to the company with the same bright color variations.

At last the visitors speak to me. "We are The O."

"You *are* travelers, who, by using circular time, visited Earth at five different centuries. Franklin, Harlan, Roosevelt, Montgomery, and Leanna, were — are — the original custodians of the message: *They are not rocks,*" I say, reminding myself to listen. More. Listen!

One of The O speaks from the shadows of his hood. "Very good. You know your history well." I try to see a face, but there doesn't seem to be one. "RUBy looks like a precious gem. Or even a simple rock, but she is much more than that. RUBy is a Crystalline, a silicon-based life-form."

I try to keep quiet. But I have a million questions. I say in spite of myself, "I knew RUBy was a being of some kind, but she never told me any details. I figured the message you gave Leanna and the others — *They are not rocks* — was a puzzle about RUBy. Now the pieces are coming together. Crystallines are not rocks!" I repeat.

"There is more," says an O. "RUBy is getting ready to go through a life process called Splitting. It is the Crystalline's way of growing and reproducing."

I try to make sense of it. "Biological life-forms consume, grow, reproduce, and eliminate waste. But," I ask The O, "how does this apply to RUBy?"

The O speak to each other before answering me. At last one of them says, "When the universe was young, the Cystallines were arrogant enough to believe that they were indestructible. They killed all carbon-based life-forms on their planet. Devastation everywhere! Their home was dying and could no longer sustain any life."

"They were able to do all of this without arms, legs, eyes, and ears?" I ask.

The O hold up a hand. "We will explain more. The Crystallines used their colors to lure space travelers. The unsuspecting visitors brought the Crystallines on board their ships. They welcomed the unlimited energy source the Crystallines offered. Before the travelers realized it, the Crystallines had taken over their ships and had set a course of conquest.

"We interceded and the Crystallines agreed to come here — with the condition that they would live passively and take no part in any acts of violence against their neighbors."

RUBy flashes yellow. The next O follows.

"A Splitting happens spontaneously every one thousand years in the life of a Crystalline. This is RUBy's seventh Splitting."

The other O continues. "RUBy needs to get back with the other Crystallines very soon. The elders will help her make a safe transition. Are you willing to help?"

"Yes," I answer. "Sure!"

"RUBy will be depending on you to be her Advocate. Don't let her down."

The O vanish.

THE CRYSTALLINES

UNCERTAINTY

MEMORY STICK
SECTOR H-7
BEING AN ADVOCATE

RUBy and I have decided that we won't tell anyone about The O's visit. But that doesn't change the fact that I've had an encounter with The O! I feel as if an army of pins is marching up my arms. The O! Should I be this happy or scared? With The O, who knows? "I'll try to be the best Advocate ever," I promise RUBy. "What does an Advocate do?"

"The O didn't tell you?"

"No."

"And you didn't ask them?"

"Well, no."

RUBy chuckles. "For Crystallines, a Splitting is as important as your birthday celebrations, graduations, marriages — all rolled into one."

"Does that mean you don't know what an Advocate does, either?" I say, so glad my buddy and I are one plus one again.

"Carlos, honestly, you're right. What *is* an Advocate?"

I raise an eyebrow. "Well, I promised The O that I would be your Advocate, and I intend to see you through this."

"Fine with me."

Houston and Leanna join us in the lounge.

Leanna and Houston order Betty Burgers. I pass. My mind is trying to figure what's expected of me as an Advocate. The lounge has a window allowing me to see the mining base. We're all thinking our own thoughts. I turn on my commpad.

"RUBy," I say. The screen flashes different shades of pink and purple, letting me know she's there.

"Miss them? I miss mine, too," RUBy says softly. Still, it was loud enough for Houston to hear. He leaps to his feet.

"Now, that's not normal," he shrieks. "Computers don't respond with feelings — not like that." Houston points an accusing finger at RUBy's screen. "What is RUBy, and don't tell me she's a computer. No way!"

"What?" I ask, faking surprise. I've known for quite some time that Houston suspects something, but he hasn't been able to figure it out. He's not going to stop this time until he's got answers. I need to make a decision . . . and fast.

"Carlos, don't lie to me, my biofe ear tells me something's up and you know it," Houston sternly says to me, sounding more serious than I've seen him before.

Leanna speaks up next. "Carlos, I'm not sure what's going on, but Houston is right. RUBy is not just a computer."

I have to protect RUBy as long as I can. Now I have to trust my friends.

Houston touches RUBy's screen cautiously, as if fearing he'll be shocked by RUBy's light flashes, or maybe something worse.

"RUBy's a computer, yet she responds independently, beyond any programming I know about. She thinks!" Houston pauses to shape his thoughts. ". . . And she seems to have real emotions. What does a computer know about *missing* anybody?"

Taking a deep breath, I answer cautiously, "What if I told you RUBy isn't a computer?"

"Well, what is she? The ship?" Houston sits down next to me and RUBy. Surprise.

"In a way. She makes the ship go. . . ."

RUBy is glowing a bright yellow, changing slowly into red. She is warning me. I suddenly realize it is not my decision alone to expose what she is.

Houston keeps the pressure on. "Carlos, since you admit to programming RUBy, I'm thinking you programmed the computer with human DNA."

I laugh sarcastically, but it sounds more hysterical than happy. I feel like a cornered lab mouse. "You flatter me," I say, trying to sound unshaken. "I'm just ten, soon to be eleven years old. How would I know how to do such a dangerous procedure? Besides, it's illegal to humanize any artificial intelligence."

"Leanna." Houston turns to her. "My biofe ear tells me Carlos is telling the truth, but he's still holding back some stuff."

"Come on, Carlos. You're a gemaginist, a genius with superior imagination," Leanna says in her big-sister friendly voice. She stands directly in front of me. "What did you create?" she says. "Should I call your dad and ask him?"

"Yeah, Wonderboy, what did you make with that superbrain of yours?" Houston shouts impatiently.

My mind races. To my surprise, RUBy speaks up. "I'll take it from here," she says, her screen flashing bright yellow.

"Computers talk, I know, I know, I know, but . . ." Houston sputters in confusion. "But RUBy sounds like she's in control. Hey, is she in charge?" he asks me.

"She's decided to speak for herself," I say, feeling relieved that RUBy has chosen to reveal her story in her own way.

MEMORY STICK
SECTOR L-10
RUBY REVEALED

"I am not the ship," RUBy says, adding, "but I make the ship go. I am not the computer, but I use the computer to communicate."

Leanna takes the screen from my hand and places it in her lap. "The way the screen changes colors has something to do with those rock things back on Atlantis," she says. "They changed colors all the time. I was working with them when The O appeared and said, *They are not rocks*. RUBy fits into all this some way, right?"

"Enough questions!" Houston blasts. "Just tell us what's up with all this."

"Show them," RUBy tells me.

"Are you sure?" I ask.

"As sure as I was about you. And that was a good decision."

"Follow me," I say, leading them into the main engine. We walk in silence. I remember the day when RUBy revealed herself to me, and I felt strong, capable of doing great things — like save RUBy from the Federation.

Just as I had on that day, a year ago, I pull a cylinder out of the floor from the center of the room. It contains a stonelike form about the size and shape of a fist. It is glowing peaceful pink, fading into purple. I hold the gem in my outstretched hand. RUBy still talked through the main computer. She seems calm.

"Let me introduce myself," says RUBy's voice, coming from the computer screens in the engineering center. "I am who you call RUBy." The entity glows pink, the same color flashing on the computer screens.

"A gemstone?" Houston asks.

"They are not rocks," Leanna whispers. Then she says it louder. "They are not rocks! That's what The O meant." Leanna studies RUBy. "When I was taking care of the gemlike stones in the Atlantis lab, The O visited and told me they were not rocks. What are you, then?"

"I am a Crystalline. Long ago, we lived on a planet far out in space, but our planet became inhospitable. Our star died, leaving us with no light source for energy. So The O transported us to Mars where we have lived for thousand and thousands of years."

I'm shocked that RUBy has told her story without a word about the aggression on the Crystallines' part. I listen carefully as she explains.

"While building the penal colony of Mars, Earth's space geologists brought back several of us. I was among them. We were unable and even a little unwilling to communicate with the Earth humans."

"I don't have to guess why!" Leanna says with a smirk.

I explain the part where I came in. "Under the direction of my father, Marcus Pace, the Federation built a fleet of ships to explore outer space. The Crystallines were tested and found to have tremendous power ranges. With them providing an endless source of energy, the ships would be invincible. My dad selected RUBy for the flagship, the fleet prototype, but RUBy refused to cooperate."

"Are you saying RUBy is a life-form, capable of making a decision like that?" Houston asks. "That would mean she is sentient."

"Exactly!" RUBy answers. "I was captured, frightened, and confused. I needed a way to communicate. So, I took a chance and trusted Carlos."

"RUBy interfaced with the ship's computer," I explained, "and together we developed a computer program to decode her colors. Making her colors into words."

"We tried to explain everything to Dr. Pace," said RUBy.

"But Dad refused to accept the science and tried to push RUBy into compliance."

Houston clapped his hands as if getting ready to gobble down a feast. "I can't wait to tell Rizin. This will solve all our problems on the Moon Colony. With a fleet of ships powered by the Crystallines, Rizin could master the stars."

"Haven't you been listening, Houston?" I say, angrily. "The Crystallines are pacifists and shun violence. If you're going to force RUBy into slavery and make her go against her code of life, just like my dad, you'll get nowhere. I promise force won't work."

"Maybe," says Rizin, standing in the doorway. "Maybe not."

MEMORY STICK
SECTOR L-11
RIZIN'S REVENGE

Oh, no. Anxiety covers me like a cape that changes into a camel spider the size of my face.

I wonder how long Rizin has been standing there. How much has he heard? What will he do with the information?

My answer comes quickly.

In one quick motion, Rizin shoves me out of the way, snatches the cylinder, and picks up RUBy with his gnarled hands. Both hands are missing several fingers. He drops her quickly, though, hopping from foot to foot and yelling, "Hot, hot, hot, HOT!"

"I thought Crystallines are supposed to be passive," says Leanna with a chuckle. She seems to enjoy Rizin being taken down by a Crystalline with a young girl's voice.

"We are not capable of doing deadly harm to anything," RUBy answers, sounding almost apologetic, "But when we are threatened, our outer skin automatically heats up to fend off aggressors. Think porcupine quills."

Rizin looks at his hands. "You've made a believer out of me," he says.

Houston comes to his aid. "Your fingers are blistering."

"Pick me up again," RUBy snaps an order. I've never heard her use our language in command mode.

Rizin is reluctant, but then he takes RUBy the Crystalline in his hands. He closes his eyes as his hands are bathed in a thick, brown color infused with shards of orange. In minutes, RUBy turns to a soft blue.

Houston studies Rizin's hands. "Wow," he says, then looking at RUBy like he'd never seen her before. Actually, none of them has ever really seen RUBy, except on the computer screen.

Houston massages Rizin's fingers and palms. His eyes widen, followed by a quick smile. "Your hands look better than before. RUBy, can you grow his fingers, too?"

Rizin's anger seems to be defused after Houston's joke.

"You see, Mr. Rizin, sir," I begin in my most respectful voice. "RUBy wasn't trying to hurt you. She was defending herself."

Rizin grunts and makes a fist. He opens the fist and stretches his fingers. Then he snaps the other gnarled hand into another powerful fist, and slowly opens it again. Rizin wiggles his loose fingers and snaps both hands into fists. "I'm top shelf," he says, adding, "just fine . . ."

Rizin abruptly turns and leaves the engine room. "Carlos," he calls over his shoulder to me. "We've got business, so set a course for Mars."

KITING
TENSION

MEMORY STICK
SECTOR Q-10
MARS PENAL COLONY

"Attention, everyone. . . . We've reached the Mars Penal Colony," RUBy announces from the bridge. She's glowing a rainbow.

"Mars . . . at last," RUBy pipes throughout the ship.

"I promised I'd get you home," I say to RUBy's computer screen. I am excited to see her mountain volcano home, too.

Looking out the window as the ship turns for a landing, I get a good view of the landscape. The prison city rests on a flat stretch called the Northern Lowlands — no hills or mountains, just orange sand and more orange sand for hundreds of miles in any direction. Other than the bright lights of the city, this part of Mars is a cold, barren, and dusty place. I guess this is why the Federation banished the cyborgs here.

We land on the roof of the colony. "WOW! I had no idea it would be laid out like this!" I say out loud.

The Mars Penal Colony was first built to hold prisoners from the Cyborg Wars. The original cyborgs arrived about fifty years ago. I studied old prison photos when I learned we were coming to Mars, and the building looked about the size of an old-fashioned portable shopping mall from the late 2000s.

"It wasn't always like this," Rizin says, shaking his head to push the bad memory out of his mind. "But cyborgs are architects, builders, every profession you can imagine. It was all in their hands: They could live in deplorable conditions or try to do better. This is their better." Rizin sounded proud of his fellow cyborgs' accomplishments.

"I'm surprised the Federation didn't stop them." Leanna magnifies the outer windows for a larger and closer view.

"The Federation doesn't care what goes on as long as nothing bothers their projects," says Rizin. He points to a part of the complex. "That's where the scientists and engineers who work on the spaceships stay."

The architecture resembles huge children's wooden toy blocks pushed together into a randomly stacked pile. The blocks appear to be made of Mars lurite, a simulated metal. Some parts of the city soar more than thirty stories, while other blocks lean on each other and still others lie side by side. The only word to describe the sight is *amazing*.

Looking a little closer out of the window, I spot at least thirty more ships similar to RUBy, all neatly parked.

Rizin touches a command menu on one of the computer screens that activates the communication to the city. "This is Rizin calling Cracker Jack Garadello."

The blank screen is replaced by the image of an older man, gray bearded, but with clear, dark eyes. According to my commhistory program, Cracker Jack Garadello is the leader of the most vicious cyborgs in the solar system. He is considered the number one enemy of the Federation and the first resident of the penal colony. He seems to have maintained his leadership role even here.

"So you made it!" says Cracker Jack, who slams his shiny, metal hands together in a raucous applause for Rizin's success. "Your informant serves you well. I got the message to have the colony and ships captured by the time you arrived."

"Everything is a go," says Rizin.

"How did you get your Federation ship to run?" Cracker Jack continues. "The crystal power rocks found on Olympus Mons volcano don't seem to perform as Dr. Pace predicted when they were first found. And he's driving us crazy trying to figure it out! Then again, he can't let us in on too much, because *we're cyborgs* and he doesn't trust us."

"Is my father here on Mars?" I blurt out.

"Is that the young Carlos Pace? So it's true you did kidnap him, Rizin, you rascal," Cracker Jack exclaims.

Rizin laughs without a hint of humor. "Believe what you want, but nobody kidnapped Carlos. He's here of his own free will."

"There are very few soldiers here because of the planned invasion of the Moon," Cracker Jack explains more. "And the other Firsts are mostly scientists and engineers. They don't have much stomach for fighting. They want to be left out of it. We've come to an agreement that they can continue to work and we won't hurt them. Yes, Dr. Marcus Pace, the boy's daddy, is here — been here for a month. What do you want me to do with him?"

"I'm going to send Carlos over with the cyborgs I brought

to command the ships. He needs to be with his father," Rizin says without hesitation.

My heart is beating so fast, I can't breathe.

"Carlos has been gone away too long." Rizin goes on making decisions about my life without including me.

"No, we will pick up Carlos and your crew in a buggy rover. We use them instead of the clunky enviro-suits," Jack says, while looking at the attendant who has brought him a tray of food.

"Please hold off," I plead with Rizin. "Will you listen to me? Please!"

"Okay. Go eat," Rizin tells Jack. "I'll get back to you in a minute or two."

"I can't go down there, even to see my father," I say desperately.

Leanna holds my hands. They are shaking. "Be calm," she whispers.

"Mr. Rizin," I begin nervously. "All of you. I promised The O that I would be RUBy's Advocate at her Splitting, something that happens to the Crystallines every thousand years."

"What? What is this gibberish?" Rizin throws up his hands.

"When did The O visit you?" Leanna asks. Her eyes show surprise.

"The other day. Two of them. They asked if I would be an Advocate for RUBy by getting her back to her home where the Splitting must take place."

"It's true what Carlos is saying," RUBy puts in. "I need to get back to Olympus — and soon."

"What is a Splitting?" Houston asks.

Rizin didn't wait for an answer. He reconnects with Jack. "I need to go to Olympus."

"What are you going to do with the boy?" Cracker Jack asks.

"I promised I'd take the kid kiting . . . near Olympus. We'll do that much. Then we'll see."

I feel somewhat relieved. I touch RUBy's screen. She is glowing a lemon yellow.

MEMORY STICK
SECTOR N-4
CARGO ROOM

Rizin explains the basic concept of kiting! Now I don't feel so good anymore. . . .

I've done some fun things before, but leaping into open sky more than twenty miles above the ground isn't one of them. *Scared* isn't the word I feel. More like *sick to my stomach*. My toes are tingling. My head is spinning. I try to imagine it being fun. Unimaginable.

Crazy cyborg FUN! Humph.

We're 'sposed to meet in the cargo room. I run to grab RUBy first, then make my way down the long spiral stairs in the engine room leading to the cargo area at the very bottom of the ship.

"Okay. Cyborg wannabes, we are going kiting today," Rizin jokingly barks at everyone.

"Sir. Yes, sir," Houston and Leanna respond, both pretending to be his soldiers.

I join in. "Don't leave me out."

"*Me*? Unknown! Advance, Me, and be recognized," Rizin says, and this time I actually feel the humor.

Seeing RUBy in my hand, Houston says, "Hey, RUBy, you never answered my question. What is a Splitting? How will it happen?"

I'm curious, too.

RUBy begins alternating wave after wave of red and white, then green and white, black and white, and on and on.

"Every thousand years, a Crystalline splits in two. Once the two parts are separated, they become complete individuals. They are what you would call identical twins. They still share identical histories, memories, equal energy, and the same power register."

"Does it hurt?" I ask, guessing that might be the job of the Advocate: to help ease the pain.

"No hurt," RUBy crushes that notion. "Each Crystalline will change over the next thousand years. RUBys number 1 and number 2 will keep their old memories, but add new ones that they experience independently. Their energy output will change as well."

"That's it?"

"It's like a birth and a big birthday splash. A major event in our lives," RUBy adds. "No reason for an Advocate, though."

"The O like mystery and suspense games," Houston says with an edge.

"I assure you this is not a game," RUBy answers quietly.

"These are your jet suits — military style," Rizin says, giving us smooth, metallic, blue-black fabric suits, helmets, gloves, and shoes for us to put on.

They have built-in commglasses that can help us see through the red dust.

My jet suit looks a lot like a kid's footed pajamas with a hood and a zipper in the front. "Frisk!"

"Not my style," says Leanna, pulling the hood over her head and face.

I put on my gloves, and, *click,* my helmet latches into place.

Rizin attaches the jet pack program to our commglasses. We are all in communication with one another, and so is RUBy, in her Crystalline form.

She flashes red, yellow, blue over and over. The three primary colors make up all the colors that regular Firsts can see.

"I guess you are excited to be going home?" I say, holding her up in my hand.

"Yes," her little girl voice chirps for all of us to hear.

"What do the color flashes mean?" Leanna wants to know.

"Supreme happiness," RUBy answers.

Then turning orange, green, and purple in succession, RUBy says, "The volcano gives us raw energy.

"Since we don't have eyes, we don't see the colors. We use the energy in light. And by manipulating the light, we create different energy that you see as color and feel as heat. Specific color and heat combinations and intensities allow us to communicate, create energy, and defend ourselves."

"Your volcano, which covers more than three hundred miles around and is sixteen miles high, is the largest volcano in our solar system," I announce.

"Trouble is," says Houston, stifling a hoot, "Carlos thinks statistics are frisk to know."

"Well, the volcano is not bigger than my home country of France," says Rizin. "I like knowing that."

All I can say is "Frisk!"

"RUBy, are you sure our ship will be fine without you on board to run it?" Rizin asks.

"I made sure our ship has more than enough power and is programmed to move around in orbit until we signal it to come to us. If boarded by someone else, it will shut down."

"Good, I will program the computer to land near our landing site. This way, we can easily get back."

MEMORY STICK
SECTOR N-6
KITING

Kiting is easy.

Just jump out of the hovering ship, spread your arms, and fly. The jet suit does the rest. The hard part is the actual jumping off the ship. I'm not sure I can do that. I can't see the ground, just a swirling, giant, dusty cloud.

"The wind will push you along like a kite as you fall to the ground," Rizin says to us.

"Looks like everyone is good for go!"

I put RUBy in my front leg jet-suit pocket and nervously move toward the cargo door. I don't think I can jump. No way.

Zap! Heat!

"Ouch, RUBy. Why'd you burn me? " I snap at her.

"Hold me so that I can feel the lights. Just don't drop me."

The Mars sky is normally clear. However, every few years, the Mars jet stream blows a foggy, brownish mix of a giant dust cloud that surrounds the top of Olympus Mons.

We are jumping at twenty-five miles up, so we will fall ten miles or so to the ground. This will take about twenty minutes.

"Don't worry, Wonderboy. Your jet suit will protect you. If bad becomes worse, we can always put you back together as a cyborg. Right?" Houston chuckles, knowing that I'm no longer afraid. I'm terrified!

Houston grabs my free hand and jumps out of the cargo doors. RUBy, in the other hand, flashes colors that I've never seen before.

"Houston, this is awesome!" RUBy chirps in our ears. "I don't get to walk, jump, or dance, so this is the ultimate."

I get to walk, jump, and dance all the time, yet this is something I've never done.

"Cyborg fun," Rizin yells. "Pure excitement!"

I look back at the ship and see Rizin holding Leanna's hand. They jump. Leanna screams.

After a minute, Houston lets go of me. "Go ahead and fly, Wonderboy."

Rizin says to me, "Stretch out your arms, twist, turn. Go for it."

Moving slowly at first, I get the hang of it quickly. The jet stream is a lot like swimming in a clear river. The current pushes me along. I can move up and down and all around.

The jet packs slow us down so that we don't fall too fast. And speeds us up when we want to go faster.

"We're approaching the dust clouds. Switch your comm-glasses to infrared heat vision and radar mode," Rizin orders. "The suits are programmed to bring you to a stop even if you can't see the ground. Thank goodness."

"WOW! This is real. I've never done anything like this before," Leanna exclaims.

Rizin was right; this really is fun! In radar mode, my comm-glasses let me see everything, even though I really can't see them with my own eyes. Leanna is moving toward me. I see her just in time to stop her from crashing into me. I reach out with both of my hands to push her away as we all continue to fall toward the volcano. I forget RUBy is in my hand!

Even though RUBy is a Crystalline, falling one mile to the ground would make her explode against the hard stones.

"Rizin!"

"Jet suits safe mode, activate now!" Rizin commands.

Leanna's, Houston's, and my suits respond to Rizin's command and the suite computers take control, slowing our speed to just a crawl.

In the same moment, Rizin stiffens his body like an arrow. His jets engage to full power blast, pushing Rizin faster to the ground.

We track him by his body heat and radar image. We all cheer when we see Rizin's right hand extend and miraculously catch RUBy. His jet pack engages at the last moment. But he's moving too fast to stop. He hits the ground, moving more than thirty miles per hour. Like with a bomb going off, a cloud of dust shoots up in the air.

We all land and quickly gather 'round him. "Rizin, are you a'right?" I call out.

A long pause.

"Rizin, are you okay?" I'm shouting louder.

A longer pause.

"Rizin!" Houston and Leanna both shout.

"Rizin!" I call again. Panic moves from my stomach to my throat. Is Rizin hurt, or worse, dead?

THE SPLITTING
ANXIETY

MEMORY STICK
SECTOR N-9
THE GATHERING

"You shouldn't do that; stop teasing them." I hear RUBy say to him in a peevish tone — so unlike RUBy.

Rizin is still floating from his kiting adventure. "So good! Landing like that is called stompin' — cyborg style!" he says, pumping his arms.

Then shifting to his commando personality, Rizin barks at us, "Okay, fun's over. Back on task."

Olympus Mons volcano is encircled by red dust clouds today. Normally the sky is clear. Rizin carries RUBy in his hands as we walk closer to the other Crystallines.

The Crystallines are dark and silent. Not a single flicker of color lights up the largest or the smallest gem.

"You're home, RUBy," I whisper as I take her from Rizin and place my friend on the ground next to the largest Crystalline I can find.

"No thanks to you, fumble fingers," Houston puts in.

"Here we go again!"

RUBy instantly flashes a bright blue-white beam, mixed with colors I've never seen.

"What's she doing?" Houston asks.

"Waking them up!" Rizin grumbles. Sometimes I don't know who is the most impatient — Rizin or Houston.

"Saying hello," I answer with my own attitude, because I have fulfilled my promise to The O. I've gotten RUBy home — with only one mishap. I shout into the stillness, "RUBy's home!"

Suddenly, a large Crystalline ignites into a clear white orb — so bright, it lights up the mountainside. I recognize the level of brightness, because RUBy often shoots similar streams of light into space all the time — no doubt communicating with her fellow Crystallines here on Mars.

Thousands of her kind join the greeting by flashing hundreds of thousands of piercing colors — so many, so intense, they blind us. We cover our eyes to stop the tangle of colors that are so noisy, I can't think.

"RUBy," I call loudly as if I need to shout over the noise the lights are creating in my head. Actually, they aren't making a sound. "RUBy, please, tone it down some."

"Oh, sorry," she tells us, cutting her intensity by half. "We do blast sometimes — especially when we're excited." RUBy slows her flickering and flashing colors, and so do the other Crystallines.

"I've never seen anything like it," says Rizin. "Fascinating."

"Can we talk to them, as we talk to you?" Leanna asks RUBy.

"Yes," she answers. "I'll try to convince White Light to agree." RUBy rapidly blinks three red, one blue, and four yellow flashes, directed at the largest of the Crystallines.

The crystal-like entity glows white, shifting into red, then yellow and several shades of purple. I have never seen RUBy talk with her own kind, so I am happy to be here, in this place.

RUBy giggles, like a little girl. "WOW! White Light will speak with you. Let me warn you. Be respectful. She's an Ancient."

RUBy goes dark. White Light shoots a blinding white shard into RUBy. She glows like a falling star. "I'm fine," RUBy explains. "White Light has downloaded the program Carlos designed for me — complete with the translator."

Yellow and red rays radiate from White Light and connect with each of our commglasses and Houston's biofe eye.

"Hay-low," says a voice that sounds like an old, old woman. "He-he-hello."

"Are we talking to the one RUBy calls White Light?" I ask.

"That requires me to say a yes," responds White Light.

Her answer makes me smile.

"This is my friend Carlos," RUBy introduces me to White Light. Out of habit, I extend my hand, then immediately wish for somebody to hack it off. Crystallines don't have arms and hands to shake. I pull my hand back and bow. "Pleased to meet you," I say, trying not to look too embarrassed.

RUBy continues to introduce us all. "These are the other ones I told you about. This is Leanna, Houston, and Rizin."

"Ah, yes, RUBy — as you call her — has shared much about you all. We thank you for bringing her back to our community. And just in time for her Splitting."

It's fascinating how fast White Light is adapting to the new communication model.

"I was visited by The O," Leanna says to White Light. "Do you know about them?"

"Of course," says White Light. She embraces us in an intense shade of emerald green. The light reminds me of a small night-light that Mom put in my room to scare off any big spiders that might be hiding under my bed. But more than that, I feel my mother's hug. Safe. Meanwhile, White Light continues.

"The O are our — the word I'm finding is — *protecting* us, no, *protect* is better. The O protect us. They understand our past, and why we reject all violent ways. The O help."

"The O visited me, too," I say proudly. "They asked me to be RUBy's Advocate. RUBy says she's never had an Advocate in her past Splittings, so why now? Why me?"

"The O do a lot of visiting," explains White Light. "They came to us saying you were coming to be RUBy's Advocate, too. We have no idea of what an Advocate is or does during a Splitting. We thought you would know."

MEMORY STICK
SECTOR M-12
THE GREAT CHANGE

RUBy is bloodred. I think something is happening. Now she is flashing like a heartbeat.

All the Crystallines are on high beam, pointing right at RUBy.

The Splitting is beginning.

I'm witnessing something that I will never see again, and I feel proud and privileged. WOW!

RUBy is pulsating red, and building heat causes her to steam. The Crystallines are shooting hot, white beams at her. Then White Light shoots a sharp light into her mass and RUBy cracks, splits down the middle, but it isn't a clean break. The two sides are not totally detached.

Instinctively, I feel the word *wrong*. "White Light, what's going on?"

"Oh, I'm so sorry. It only happens one in a million times. When the Splitting is not complete, the Crystalline burns out and we lose them."

"They die?" Leanna shouts. Her voice has a hysterical sound, the same thing I am feeling. RUBy can't die.

"What can be done?" I ask.

"Nothing," says White Light.

"They have no arms, legs," Rizin says, as if thinking out loud.

I get it, what Rizin means. The Crystallines *can't* help complete the Splitting. But I can. I grab RUBy, at the same time White Light yells, "No-o-o-o, Carlos!, You'll be burned whole and complete."

The pain is as bad as the Topas Making. I survived that, I'll survive this. I snap RUBy in two and toss the two pieces on the ground. My hands are burned beyond recognition.

All I remember hearing before I collapse is White Light telling my friends, "Put his hands on me."

When I wake, I have two healed hands. No pain or memory of it.

"Wonderboy," Houston teases, "I thought you were going to join the cyborg team with two artificial hands. But you got lucky. You did good."

"I don't know if you're smart, lucky, brave, or stupid," says Leanna. "But I'm glad you're okay. RUBy is, too."

That's what I wanted to hear. "RUBy, there are two sides of you now. Which one is you?"

"Each side is equal until you choose. Then I begin my new life," they answer as one voice.

I pick up RUBy and announce, "This is RUBy One, and I am her Advocate. Partners until the end."

"Now we know what an Advocate is," says White Light.

I watch as Rizin anxiously paces back and forward. Stopping, he puts his finger to his forehead. "There is a reason for this," Rizin says. "The O don't tell us what to do; they give us clues that put us on a course of action that could lead to a variety of outcomes. *Advocate* is a clue."

I wonder where he is going with this angle of reasoning. I listen quietly. It isn't easy.

Rizin smoothly analyzes the situation. "Carlos, you just showed us that without legs, arms, and the ability to move, the Crystallines are limited. Why did they call Carlos an Advocate? I've asked myself. The O made sure Carlos was here to use his hands to save RUBy's life."

Houston chimes in. "I just looked it up on my commglasses. *Advocate* means to support, to intercede on behalf of another. So what else were The O telling us?"

I hop in with, "Ideally, the Crystallines need help from an entity with arms and legs. . . ."

"A close friendship . . ." Leanna adds.

"I'm thinking more of a symbiotic relationship — two species who live in close and mutually beneficial association," says Rizin.

"Carlos and RUBy are a perfect example of how symbiosis works," says Houston. "RUBy runs the ship and defends it, and Carlos gives her mobility and the means to communicate cross species."

"White Light," Rizin begins carefully, "what would you think of this offer? We cyborgs pledge to be Advocates of the Crystallines and vice versa. You power our ships and we will give you mobility."

White Light goes dark while a color spectacular flashes around us. At last, the Ancient one turns red, then orange. "There are some who agree and some who don't. So, I will allow for volunteers. Take those who flash green. Then we will see how this symbiosis works. It seems right to me, somehow." White Light glows brighter than ever. "One thing," she adds. "No Crystalline is allowed to provoke a violent act or react to any situation with force."

"But . . ."

White Light shuts off. The mountain goes dark.

We've arrived back at the penal colony, completely space wild with excitement about our time with the Crystallines. So why does Rizin have to mess up the good feelings by insisting that I go see Dad over in the Federation building?

"It's not that I don't love my parents. I do." But if I go over there, he'll make me stay and I want to see RUBy, Houston, and Leanna get their day in court. "I'd like to talk to him," I say.

Rizin agrees.

We use untraceable commglasses so our location can't be tracked. Actually, we're right down the hallway.

"Dr. Pace, this is Li Rizin, Moon Base mining manager. . . ."

"I know who you are," snaps Dad in his no-nonsense voice. "Where is my son?"

"Carlos is well, unharmed, safe."

"I'll be the judge of that when you bring my son home."

"I wanted you to know, Carlos has been in good care. No one has hurt him, and I think he has learned a lot. He's a very special kid. I'm very proud of him."

"That's just what I'm worried about. What has he learned that you people would be proud about?" Only Dad would say something that dumb and wonder why it made the other person angry. Rizin handles it well.

"You'd be surprised about what we people have to offer," says Rizin. "Here is your son."

"Dad," I say, trying to sound upbeat.

"Carlos, are you okay?" he asks.

"I'm good. You sound good. How's Mom? Have you been getting my weekly comm-messages?"

"They've kept your mother and me sane, but they're not enough. We miss you and we want you home!"

"I miss you, too," I say, feeling good that my father seems changed. "I want to come home, but I am part of something that is beyond my imagination."

"Your mind is so advanced, yet you are still just a kid, an impressionable kid." Uh-oh, Dad's beginning to sound like Dad. "They are not like you. Can't you feel it?"

"Rizin is our leader, and he's tough, but fair," I say. "Houston is a cyborg. Leanna is a clone, but they're my best friends. RUBy is a Crystalline, and she just went through a Splitting. Happens every thousand years . . . and . . ."

"Carlos," Dad yells. "Stop running your sentences together. And don't talk to me about those cyborg thugs and misfits. What about that rock you call RUBy? How did you get the rock to work?" he asks.

"I asked!"

"What?" He didn't get it.

"Dad, I finally have the proof that RUBy is a sentient being. She's a Crystalline. . . ."

"Stop that foolishness. A rock can't be a sentient being."

"Dad, you're so wrong."

"And you're disrespectful. Those creatures you're with . . ."

"Don't call them names, Dad. They are my friends. Not at all what you think."

"Friends! They've got you brainwashed. But don't worry. They will be caught. When you get home, you're going to an attitude adjustment counselor. You just hold on, son. We are going to get you back soon."

How come Dad can't be like other fathers and say we'll share a swifting game when I come home, instead of sending me to an attitude adjustment counselor?

"Just so, Dad," I agree, fearing I might turn this into one of our usual screaming matches. "Tell Mom I love her. I study every day, and I exercise and eat well, too. Honest, I'm fine."

I disconnect my commglasses and go find my friends.

MEMORY STICK
SECTOR N-14
WAR DRUMS

We are in a food shop on the penal side of the colony. I'm telling Houston and Leanna about the talk I had with my dad. "He hasn't changed," I say. "He's still a Wholer with a doctorate degree."

Unexpectedly, the T activates. The screen saver, a picture of the Taj Mahal, dissolves and a voice calls our attention:

"An emergency announcement from the chancellor will start in one minute."

A full image of the chancellor appears.

"My fellow citizens," Taylor Graham begins. *"I come to you with a troubled heart, saddened even more by recent events."* The chancellor's face hardens and his eyebrows move together as if in pain.

"Liar!" Other cyborgs in the room shout out at the image on the T monitor.

"The World Federation of Nations defense forces, our proud and courageous soldiers, were planning a new age for mankind, a new age of space exploration. Our marine explorers have a long history. They built the Moon Base and Jupiter

string space stations. Now they have a new fleet of ships to take us to places beyond our solar system."

The chancellor proudly pulls himself tall the way I figure he did when he was a space marine general.

"All of our efforts for this new age of mankind have come to a sudden and painful halt." He raises his hands and counts with his fingers to three as he continues. *"The spaceships don't work. The cyborgs have gone crazy. And clones don't want to work."*

The chancellor breaks the serious mood with a small chuckle. Then his face stiffens again, looking angry. *"We will not lose our future to a bunch of crazy cyborg thugs and lazy clones. I've been more than gracious, patient, and tolerant. Enough is plenty."*

Everyone in the food shop is completely silent. I am still for a minute. This felt like getting yelled at by my dad.

"For our peaceful and beautiful world to work, we all must be accountable.

"Firsts lead humanity forward.

"Cyborgs adapt and overcome.

"Clones sustain and make our world work.

"Each role is important. By working together and staying in our appointed roles, we make ours a better world. The great leader Booker T. Washington described our world the best. We are like the hand with each finger working separately and as one hand when necessary.

"You, my fellow cyborgs, better known as Moonborgs. Stop the madness and all will be forgiven. Surrender the Moon and

return to normal work and play. Do this and no one, and I mean no one, will be punished.

"As for The Liberty Bell and this so-called freedom movement, it will end now. There will be no trial. For those who admit guilt and swear allegiance to The WF of N, all will be forgiven for you, too."

I look at Houston and then to everyone else in the store. Was the chancellor going to make it this easy?

"I'm extending the hand of friendship to anyone who is willing to take it. But as the chancellor, I cannot tolerate any further disobedience. We will move forward with or without. I've ordered the space marines to attack the Moon Colony in the next eighteen hours. Make up your minds. Thank you to all."

The screen goes blank.

Rizin leaps to his feet. "That's what I needed," he shouts. clenching his fists. "Graham says eighteen hours. His marines will be here in ten hours. And we've got to be ready."

TALKING BAD
TENSION

MEMORY STICK
SECTOR M-8
HOUSTON FLIES

The chancellor didn't get one taker.

Rizin assigns his cyborg captains to each of the twenty operational Federation spaceships. Then he gives each one a Crystalline.

"These are not rocks," Rizin begins. "They are easily mistaken for rocks, disrespected, and dismissed, but they are Crystallines, a sentient life-form. They live on light and produce energy. They have agreed to work with us by powering our ships. We, in turn, will give them the ability to move."

As Rizin talks, the captains stand taller and pull their shoulders back farther.

"Take care of your Crystallines," Rizin commands. "Treat them with respect and kindness and demand the same for yourselves. In this relationship, you are both equal and free."

You'd have to see the twenty captains all lined up, shoulder to shoulder, to appreciate the power of the moment. Each cyborg captain holds his or her helmet under one arm, and the other outstretched hand, with palm up, holds a Crystalline. I give Epps a victory signal. Tools and Sticks are commanding a ship together.

Colors dance around their heads like halos. Leanna wipes a tear from her eye. Rizin is visibly moved, especially when the captains snap to attention as he passes them during inspection. The captains promise to be good Advocates.

But we all cheer when Rizin tells Houston to join the captains. He is given a Crystalline, RUBy's other half. To see him standing there with RUBy Two in his palm makes me burst into applause and yo-shouts. "Yo, Houston. Yo, Houston. Yo, Houston!" Soon others joined me in my spirited display of pride. "Yo, Houston. Yo, Houston . . ." It feels good to cheer for my friend — the one who teases me — my good friend — the one who taunts me. He's still okay with me.

The next few hours we work steady to get the Crystallines installed on the Federation ships. Couldn't help but think how Dad could have gotten the same results, but he was unable to say a simple *please*. Bad.

The Crystallines choose a computer voice and a name. I've especially enjoyed watching Houston bond with RUBy Two. She sounds a little older than RUBy, but in all other ways, they are the same — for now.

Big House checks in. "We're ready on the Moon!"

"See you soon," says Rizin, who orders the captains to man their ships. They are in battle mode — tight, light, and flying with minimum crew.

"We'll be ready when they try to sneak up on us," Leanna says.

"Remember. Courage defeats the impossible," Rizin shouts our battle cry.

"Courage defeats the impossible," the team answers.

MEMORY STICK
SECTOR Q-4
SURPRISE ATTACK

"All hands to battle," Rizin broadcasts to the entire ship. "The space marines have attacked Shackleton ahead of time, just as we suspected they would."

I never undressed, so I'm one of the first to reach the bridge. "RUBy, magnify the command center on Shackleton."

In an instant, I am in the middle of chaos. Everyone is running around, giving orders and commanding the city's computers to operate. The marine ships hit the city hard. Our Crystallines could wipe them out with one blast. Twenty blasts could take out the whole planet.

"I'd like to know what Rizin is planning." I think out loud.

"Our goal is to keep Leanna safe until she goes to court," Rizin says. "My plan is to wipe out the Federation ships, then demand that Chancellor Graham grant Leanna her trial."

"But, but," I stammer. "You promised White Light that the Crystallines would not participate in violence . . . and, and, now." I freeze.

"Stop babbling, Carlos," Rizin snaps at me like an angry bear. "I can hear the fear in your words. This is not the time to be dim. I need you to be as bright as you can be."

"Rizin, I'm not sure what you have planned, but the Crystallines won't be involved with anything violent. The space marines easily outgun us without the Crystallines' help. I calculate they will take Shackleton in a matter of ten minutes if we do nothing," says Big House.

"Hold on," Rizin says, raising his hand before giving Big House the word.

He turns to me and grabs my shoulders. "Carlos, I need you to imagine how we can win without using violence, yet fulfill our goals. I don't care how crazy it is, just use that gemaginist brain. I will count to ten, and you need to give me an answer."

"One." He starts to count.

My mind races. I don't want to let him down.

"Two seconds . . . three seconds."

How do we stop the attack? Soldiers have to attack even if they don't want to. I need to make them unable to fight. How do I make them unable to fight?

"Four."

Make them go to sleep? Make them hungry? No, I need to distract them. Get them to look at something else. Something important.

"Five."

I can give them something they want. A present. Yes, a present; everyone likes a present.

"Six seconds . . . seven seconds."

What present do they want? They want to win. How do we let them win the war and we get what we want, all without fighting?

"Eight. Nine seconds. Ten seconds, Carlos. Time's up. Tell me now."

"White Light didn't say you couldn't *talk* about being violent," I say with a big grin as I repeat my plan. "The space marines think we are fully loaded and ready to fire. They don't know the Crystallines are totally nonviolent. I say, use your negotiation skills to make the Federation think they are winning, by offering them a gift, their own ships."

Rizin nods in understanding. "Kid, you amaze me." Then speaking to Big House, he says, "We're coming. Be ready to dance with me."

MEMORY STICK
SECTOR Q-5
A PRESENT

"Space command, stop your attack. We surrender!" Big House announces to the marine ships blasting away at his Moon city.

The X-destroyers instantly stop the attack.

"Governor Big House, this is General Jabar Ismuth." I hear his voice clearly in the commglasses attached to my jumpsuit helmet. "I'm glad you decided to stop this temper tantrum. We will land immediately."

"I think not," says Rizin, leading all twenty ships into combat position — in clear view, but just out of range of the older X-destroyers. We must look awesome, hovering in battle formation.

"Power down or be annihilated," Rizin says. "We are fully powered and ready to strike."

"Big House just told me on secure commglasses that everything is being broadcast to Earth," Leanna says, covering a smile. "I don't think the general knows the whole world is listening."

"Wait, General Ismuth." Rizin's voice is heard by all of us. "We have a present for you."

"Rizin, I should have known," the general answers back.

"We will surrender the ships and I will turn myself in, if you allow us to speak directly to the chancellor."

A pause.

"What if we refuse your offer and take the ships? We have three times the number of ships you have. Our men are better trained, and we have greater firepower. What are you using to power your ships? I understand that's why they haven't been used before. So we're to believe that in a couple of days, you've been able to do what Federation scientists haven't been able to do yet? No way. This is some kind of trick. A trap, maybe."

"I thought you might think that way," Rizin says calmly. "But these new ships are faster than your clunky X-destroyers. They can dodge your plasma weapons long enough to send a plasma-gush-beam toward your engines. Your vessels will explode with the force of a sun. You and your fleet will be blown into a billion particles of dust."

Another period of silence.

"General Ismuth, I'm waiting," Rizin says, pretending to be patient.

More time. I figure General Ismuth is talking to his superiors, who are trying to get to the chancellor.

"Nice present, isn't it?" Rizin continues to badger. "We talk to the chancellor and we give you back your ships intact. You refuse and we blow you away in five minutes."

"Let's settle this in court," Big House addresses General Ismuth. "We can save a lot of lives. I can speak for all the cyborgs here on the Moon: We will abide by the court's decision."

MEMORY STICK
SECTOR Q-7
WAR OR PEACE

I never thought I'd be happy to see Chancellor Graham. RUBy's been very quiet since we've left Mars. She's been worried about how easy it is to fall into violent ways. "You've been peaceful beings for centuries," I say for encouragement.

"But I know how easy it is to . . ."

"How so?"

"I'm enjoying myself a little too much," RUBy responds. I can feel the embarrassment in her words and her dark blue color. "The truth is, I'm excited about meeting the space marines and showing off our skills," RUBy explains.

"Hey, I'm your Advocate. I won't lead you into violence unless it's in self-defense. Okay?"

"Okay."

The chancellor and Rizin meet as holographs at the Moon's operational center. We watch via our commglasses. General Ismuth, Big House, and Toby are also present at the talks.

Rizin sternly looks around the room, then turns back to the

chancellor's holograph. "All we want is to settle this in court. We don't have to fight," begins Rizin.

The chancellor ignores Rizin and speaks to Big House. "Thank you for putting your crazy dog Rizin back on his leash. You do know he's a cyborg terrorist. He needs to be banished to Mars with the rest of the crazy cyborgs."

"Terrorists blow things up, instead of talking in court," Big House coolly responds to the chancellor's harsh words about his friend. "Is your position so unjust that you can't handle a fair trial?"

The chancellor points his finger at Rizin while speaking to Big House. "How do we know he won't pull another temper tantrum if he doesn't get his way?"

"How do we know you won't do the same?" Big House says. He ignores the change on the chancellor's face and hurries on. "The fifteen judges at the World Supreme Court can only be called together by the chancellor. You have stalled and stalled. Now we want action."

"What do you hope to prove?" The chancellor stands abruptly. "Clones are domestic animals, and cyborgs are metal-heads. We all know this. Let's not waste time. We need to put all the cyborgs back on Mars and forget about them."

Rizin clasps his hands. "I know you are a selfish man, Graham. So let's make this easy for you. Do you want to remain chancellor or start a needless war in which your fleet is destroyed and so are your new spaceships that we know how to power? Think about that."

The chancellor snarls at Rizin. "Fine, I will summon the court to convene! One week. Don't be late. Leanna and Houston will be allowed to leave the Moon; bring the boy Carlos. And you, Rizin, will be under arrest when you get here."

"Agreed, I will also send Toby, a Federation officer, to escort them on one of the new ships. The rest of the ships will remain in orbit around the Moon." Big House commands, not allowing the chancellor to comment.

Frisk.

Computer, command end.

THE TRIAL
PERFECTION

MEMORY STICK
SECTOR M-3
AT YOUR COMMAND

The worst part of the journey back to Earth is knowing we'd be separated. As soon as we land at the Federation Complex, Rizin, Houston, and Leanna are taken into custody. They release me to my mother, who takes me home in spite of my resistance.

The house looks the same — everything in its place. Smells the same — something good steaming up the kitchen. Tastes the same — Mom's beef stew, my favorite. Mom's homemade biscuits are so delicious; I tease her, saying, "I don't know who ate all those biscuits. I think they were so light and fluffy, they just floated away."

She laughs and that feels more like home than anything. "Carlos, you're really here," she says. "I've been worried sick about you."

I continue eating quietly. Mom watches me with a fixed smile. Then we both start to talk at the same time.

"You go on, Mom. . . ."

"I was just going to say how much I appreciated the comm-messages you sent us, otherwise I would have been out of my mind with worry."

I wouldn't dare tell her that I'd programmed my comm-glasses to send automatic messages once a week, telling her I was okay and not to fret. "I'm glad they helped."

"Your father will be home soon," she says. "He will be so happy to see you, too."

I shrug and throw my hand up to block her words.

"And what does that little gesture mean?" Mom asks, clearly upset.

"Mom, I don't want to get into it with Dad. He refuses to listen, even though he knows the truth," I say.

Mom comes back with, "What? Like RUBy is a sentient being?"

"Yes, as a matter of fact. RUBy looks like a rock, but she is a being with a history that everybody will know about very soon. I wish Dad had looked at the facts as a real scientist. The Crystallines are a much greater discovery than forcing a new and different life-form into slavery. He's better than that."

Mom doesn't tell me to stop being foolish and stubborn anymore. She calms down and begins asking me questions about RUBy, my friends, and what proof I had that RUBy is sentient. "I want to hear your story," Mom says. "And I'm going to listen as your mother and not a biophysicist."

I can't help but show my excitement. If I can get Mom to listen, then I'll have a better chance of persuading Dad.

I spend the rest of the evening sharing my memory stick with Mom. First, she virtually meets Leanna and feels some of the pain of a clone Making — not in full force, but enough to get an idea of how horrible a Making is. Mom marches in a protest demonstration with Houston, Rizin, and Epps for equal rights for cyborgs. Mom fights her way out of the Topas Corporation to save Leanna and Houston and escapes to the Moon. Then she goes kiting on Mars and experiences the greeting of the Crystallines, and meets White Light.

"So, The O are real!" Mom exclaims. "I always thought they were fictional — like the Greek and Roman gods. But they're for a fact and they've made you an Advocate?" Mom says proudly. "I am surprised."

"Say you'll help my friends," I plead. "They aren't prepared to present their cases. They'll need our help. Is there a way to use your influence to get me in to see them?"

"Carlos, trust me. Your friends will do fine," Mom says. "There are lots of people who are sympathetic to their cause."

I study Mom's face. She's hiding something from me. I can tell by the way she plays with her fingers.

"Besides," she goes on. "I can't get involved because of your father's position. What would it look like for the wife and son of the director of the Federation Space Program to defend clone and cyborg freedom and equal rights?"

"I think it would be great if we took a stand for what is right, Mom. You've taught me that all my life. Now you're the one backing off?

"At first, I was only interested in getting RUBy back to Mars where she could live happily among her kind," I explain. "But Houston, Leanna, and all the others have opened my eyes to how clones and cyborgs are treated."

"I know that," says Mom. "I understand more than you think."

What is Mom really saying? Was she . . . I turn to face her. "Where is Three Nines?" She's our domestic clone.

Mom fumbles with her ring. "I, I, sold her. I didn't need her anymore."

"Are you a secret member of The Liberty Bell?"

"Never. What makes you think such a thing?"

"Okay. I was just wondering, because you don't talk like Dad, who thinks all cyborgs are brutes and all clones are stupid."

"You don't have to belong to The Liberty Bell to know those ideas are extreme — except the Wholers."

"Like Dad," I put in.

Mom didn't answer. I still felt like she wasn't telling me her real feelings.

Sleeping in my own bed was as great as the pancakes I devoured for breakfast.

"Get dressed," Mom says in her professional voice. "We've got places to go, people to see, and problems to solve. So I'm gonna need all the help I can get. How 'bout you, brother? Could you give me a hand?"

I chime in the chorus of the oldie-but-goodie song. "I'm gonna need all the help I can get. . . ."

Then together, we belt out, "How 'bout you, brother? Could you give me a hand?"

I haven't seen Mom this playful in a long time. I like her this way.

I have no idea where we are going until we get here. Mom parks our farcar in front of the Federation prisoner holding station. "You did it!" I shout. "You are so special."

"I couldn't get those memory sticks and diaries out of my head. I'm not sure about clones and cyborgs. Things have always been this way, but I do think we might need to change. Especially when I've seen and heard The O as you have."

Mom has gotten permission to visit with the prisoners under the pretense that she is doing research. She cleared me as her son.

"Okay, I've gotten you in here," Mom whispers. "Do what you need to do and let's go."

I am so glad to see my friends. We all greet one another — all talking at the same time. Each one expressing his concern for the other and the joy of being together once again.

"Where's Leanna?" I ask.

"The women's section," Rizin says.

"Have you seen my brother, Toby?" Houston asks.

"No," I say. Then turning to Mom, I apologize. "Mom," I say. "This is Li Rizin and Houston Ye. This is my mother, Dr. Penelope Pace. She's helping us."

"How do you do, gentlemen? But, no, I am not helping here," Mom says with a laser-sharp glare at me. "I'm observing you for a research project. That is all."

"Understood," Rizin says. "We appreciate what you did to get our friend Carlos here. He is a valued member of our team."

"He is a child! My son!" Mom snaps. "And he should have been put off that ship as soon as you realized he was ten years old!" Then reeling her emotions in a bit, she says calmly, "I thank you for treating Carlos well. But, you must understand my feelings as a parent."

"Understood again," Rizin says.

"Mom doesn't get it. You're like family. And I'll do what I can for you," I say.

"Right now we need a lawyer," says Rizin. "A good one."

"Leanna mentioned her best friend's uncle, attorney Benjamin Jaffe," Houston adds.

"He's one of the best constitutional lawyers in the Federation. He's also expensive," Mom whispers. "If we can get him, you'd be set." Mom walks toward the door. It is time to go.

I wonder, does Mom realize what she said: *if we can get him . . .? We.* She's furious at Rizin on one hand, then on the other hand, includes herself in the hunt for a good lawyer. *Okay, Mom, what's up?*

"Tell Leanna that we're pulling for her, her mom, and Dr. Ayala," I say.

MEMORY STICK
SECTOR QE-2
COURT DAY

Mom gets us permission to meet to plan our case with Houston, Leanna, Rizin, Dr. Ayala, and Annette. If necessary, one of us will have to present the testimony, because we still don't have a lawyer. Then one afternoon, Mom comes to our drab little room on the lower level of the prison. She has a red-headed man with unusual dark eyes in tow. "This is Ben Jaffe," she almost squeals. "He's agreed to be our lawyer."

"We don't have any money," I speak right up.

"This is pro bono."

August 9, 2171

"Hurry up!" I say while running ahead of Mom, through the main gate of the Peace Palace, home of the World Supreme Court. Reaching back, I pull my mother's hand to speed her up. "Come on. You seem to be walking in a daze," I nag.

"Carlos, don't you realize you're standing in front of an architectural masterpiece that represents ancient ideas that are still as fresh as this morning . . . peace, freedom, and justice?

Take a moment to savor it all," she says, staring at the building's clock tower and giant stained-glass windows.

"I know, Mom," I say impatiently. "This is the Peace Palace, built by Andrew Carnegie back in 1907. I don't want to be late."

"Carlos, stop. We are twenty minutes early," Mom says in her mother-in-charge voice. "I want you to look at the beautiful rose garden, oak trees, and even the rocks on the ground. This is special."

Mom squeezes my hand a little bit, getting my attention. "Just because you're smart doesn't mean you're grown up. The decisions that are to be made here today are going to impact our world in ways we can only imagine. Billions of people are going to be watching us on the T."

I get what Mom is saying. I hadn't thought about the whole world watching. A big burst of wind almost throws us off balance. Mom gives my black, unruly hair a brush with her hand.

"Dr. Pace and Carlos, we've been expecting you," one of the guard officers greets us. "Please follow me to the witness waiting area."

Mom takes another look at me, straightens my tie, and brushes lint off of my jacket. After a moment, she calmly says, "Okay? Ready."

I flash Mom a silly, cartoonish grin. "If I gotta!" I can always make her smile when I do that. It doesn't fail me this time.

"Stop being devilish," Mom says, stifling a laugh.

I'm so glad Mom's with us, I think as we walk in solemn silence into the palace where we are embraced by tradition, protocol, and honor.

Court officers and other very important world officials are standing around in the halls. I eavesdrop, picking up bits and pieces of conversations about the proceedings — some pro, some con. One man expresses himself emphatically. "I think clones are paper products, as opposed to Firsts, who are the real china."

Another woman argues that she feels clones and cyborgs should have the right to compete for jobs and education on a level playing field. Meanwhile, I hear a person say, "I believe clones were created to be our servants. What would they do without us to take care of them?"

"There are eleven million clones in existence at any given time. Who's going to do all the work they do?"

I don't know what is going to happen today, but I know there are a lot of people with conflicting ideas. I'm glad I'm here. I only wish Dad could be here with us, too.

My spirits drop when I see Joe Spiller standing by a side door. Mom told me earlier, the chancellor had promoted Joe Spiller to secretary of code enforcement, a new planetary position he'd created. With Spiller is a hideous biobot. As I pass it, the creature hisses nastily. Spiller pulls its chain. My toes tingle.

Our escort ushers us into a small sitting room with nineteenth-century antique furniture. Suddenly, I hear the sound of a low growl. I turn in anticipation. It's Apache wagging his tail. "Come, big guy," I say, challenging the wolf. Houston and Toby have arrived in the room. Mom's about to faint, until I explain to her it's Houston's Familiar. She still isn't happy about being so near a wolf — biograph or not!

"Hello, Dr. Pace. Good to see you." Houston speaks to Mom, then turns to me. "So you made it, little bro." Houston gives me a fake jab to the chest. A big, generous grin spreads across his face. I'm thinking he genuinely is glad to see me.

I shove my hands in my pockets, trying to look a little older.

A side door opens and a court officer escorts us to the witness seats. "Everyone to your seats. The justices will arrive soon," says Mr. Jaffe. Houston taps his shoulder to call in Apache. We are so fortunate to have Mr. Jaffe, Sandra's uncle. She convinced him to take the case to help Leanna, her best friend. Sandra's parents disowned Mr. Jaffe when they found out he was having anything to do with The Liberty Bell conspirators.

Then the defendants enter the court, Dr. Anatol Ayala, Dr. Annette Deberry, and Leanna Deberry, and they take their seats next to us.

In the same instant, Mr. Jaffe activates his biograph of our second lawyer, John Quincy Adams, former United States president and congressman.

I think it is a smart move to use the aid of Mr. Adams in building our argument. There hasn't been a lot of time to develop this case, but I hope we are convincing. The real winners are those who have changed their attitudes about clones and cyborgs and are willing to give them equality under the law.

"Mr. Adams, are you ready, sir?" Mr. Jaffe questions the biograph.

"Indeed, I'm ready for the cause of justice," the biograph answers.

"All rise. The court now sits," says the court clerk, standing in front of the judges' table.

The room instantly becomes quiet. Fifteen chief justices from fifteen nations enter the room from a side door leading to their chairs at a table in the front of the court room. Argentina, Brazil, Canada, Chile, China, Great Britain, Israel, Italy, Japan, Kenya, Russia, South Africa, Syria, Turkey, United States. "They serve by lottery for eight-year terms," Mom explains.

I can't help but notice that they look so stern and serious. I'd like to make a cartoonish grin at one of them to see if he or she could resist laughing. I'd do it, except Mom would have a fall-down fit if I did.

In unison, the justices — while still standing — raise their right hands and begin: "I solemnly declare that I will perform my duties and exercise my powers as judge honorably, faithfully, impartially, and of good conscience." They sit down.

The president of the court, who is the chief justice of Japan, Hanna Nagishana, hits her black gavel on the long, rectangular-shaped, real mahogany table. The loud banging echoes throughout the hall.

"What are they doing?" Houston asks me. "Don't they have lie detectors in this court?"

"This is a used-to-be. It has always been done, so they do it, anyway, they also have detectors." I whisper back.

"Everyone, please be seated. Counsel, please state your oath," Justice Nagishana says. There is pure authority in her voice.

The lawyers stand and raise their right hands. "I solemnly declare that I will perform the duties incumbent upon me as an official of The World Federation of Nations Supreme Court with loyalty, discretion, and good conscience, and that I will faithfully observe all the rules of the court."

"I object, Your Honors," says Mitch Thomas, lead lawyer for the United States Department of Justice team. His voice is tough, but his round face, matching belly, and rosy cheeks give him a Santa Claus appearance — almost likeable. But his looks should not fool you. He's tough.

Ben Jaffe laughs, mildly amused. "We haven't started yet, what are you objecting to?" he asks Thomas.

Mr. Thomas ignores Mr. Jaffe. "Justices, a computer doesn't have a conscience. It can't swear the oath it just stated." The lawyer points at Mr. Adams.

Before anyone has a chance to speak, Chief Justice Nagishana calmly says to Mr. Thomas, his team of five lawyers, and everyone in the courtroom, "This matter has already been settled. Both sides can use any tools they want. A computer is a tool, and so is a biograph. This court recognizes Mr. Benjamin Jaffe as the legal counsel on this case, and the court will address Mr. Jaffe only. Do you all understand? We will continue without interruption, please."

"Yes, Chief Justice," both lawyers say, moving back to their seats.

The clerk steps forward. "Please notice the lights above my desk. These lights are connected to the audio and visual recording computers. Red means the person speaking isn't being completely truthful, while green indicates the person is telling the truth."

I think this is so frisk.

Bang!

Bang!

Bang!

Chief Justice Nagishana hits the gavel, capturing everyone's attention. "Please rise," she says. Dr. Ayala struggles a bit to stand, with help from Dr. Deberry. "It is not the charge of this court to prove anyone's guilt or innocence, but to hear arguments regarding the abuse of humans protected by the Universal Declaration of Human Rights and other civil rights guarantees granted by your resident country, the United States."

The chief justice tells the Federation lawyer to begin his opening statement.

"According to the Justice Department of the World Federation of Nations, Dr. Anatol Ayala and Dr. Annette Deberry have broken numerous laws by creating an illegal infant clone, passing her off as a human, and organizing a subversive group known as The Liberty Bell to start a rebellion against the Federation. Their claim is that our laws are unjust and therefore invalid. We intend to prove that Drs. Ayala and Deberry are incorrect in their assumption that laws written by and for humans should be applied to nonhumans."

A knot forms in my stomach and I close my eyes to fight back the need to yell out my feelings. I'd like to tell Mr. Thomas that he and all his lawyers wouldn't know *truth* if it crawled up their arms and bit them.

"Mr. Jaffe, we will hear from you next."

"Quite the contrary to what's been said," begins Ben Jaffe, in a perfectly measured way, "we base our argument on a question: What is a human? We believe that answer will lead this court to agree that our laws must be reinterpreted to include other sentient life-forms."

Mr. Thomas gets to present his case first. As might be expected, his team is well prepared and organized. Leanna is called as a witness.

"Did your mother, Annette Deberry, trick you into believing you were a human?" Mr. Thomas asks, glaring at her.

We know Mr. Thomas is going to be hard on her. Leanna practiced answering questions with Houston and me. So she is prepared. "No, my mom didn't trick me." The light flashes green.

"Let me rephrase: Did Dr. Deberry tell you that you were a clone before you started school?"

"No, she did not." Again the light flashes green.

"Did she lie and tell you she was your mother?"

"My mom didn't lie to me." The light flashes red. "I mean she is my mother. I don't care what you say." The light flashes green.

"And how old are you, Leanna?"

"Fourteen."

"Your Honors, as you can see, the clone is confused, defiant, and clearly malfunctioning. The law is very simple: A person cannot make an infant clone because it has a life expectancy of thirteen to fourteen years old. It is cruel to bring it into existence and then watch it die at such an early age." He gives Annette a disgusted smirk. "Our clone laws have a purpose — they are compassionate and for the common good. Nobody can break the law or change it because they don't like it."

Mr. Ben Jaffe surveys the room before he begins. "Let us first question, why is it illegal to create a clone? The truth is, in the early stages of development, the rapid cell growth lowered the life expectancy of an infant clone to age thirteen years or so. Outlawing the process of infant cloning seemed the compassionate thing to do at the time. There is no problem with the initial decision and subsequent law."

Jaffe stands in the middle of the courtroom. He looks taller and more confident than ever. "But very few people know that the formula was improved and the life of a clone could be expanded to that of any healthy human being. The Topas Corporation said the formula didn't work and began making adult — altered — clones. Even now, when clones have been in service for thirteen years, they are terminated. Note: Topas holds a monopoly on the creation and sale of adult clones, which is legal, but if infant cloning is allowed, they will have no business. Think of the lives that would be saved."

Go, Jaffe! Go, Jaffe! Talk about a one, two, gotcha! Mr. Jaffe delivered a one-two knockout. Let's see Thomas argue that.

"What proof do you have to support these allegations about one of the world's corporate leaders?" the justice from Russia asks. "Beware of slander. It has a mean bite."

Jaffe speaks up immediately, "Leanna is fourteen and she has no signs of deterioration. She's healthy, athletic, and does very well academically. She's like any other girl her age. She was made with the stabilizing formula her great-grandfather developed."

Jaffe holds an old book over his head. "This is The Father of Cloning, Dr. Montgomery's diary. In it, he tells how he offered his stabilizer to the Topas Corporation, but they didn't use it. It would cut into their profits. They thought they had stolen his work, but he managed to save it and put it in safe hands. That's why we have it today. We are killing people for no reason other than profit. I fail to see the compassion and the common good in that."

Thomas takes over. "Infant cloning, adult cloning, with formula or without, doesn't matter. Clones are not people. They are manufactured beings. It's clearly stated in the US Supreme Court case of *Diamond v. Chakrabarty* in 1980 and the *Ficher v. State of California* in 2066. 'If the biological material is manufactured, cannot reproduce itself, has an unnatural life span, the mass is considered patentable and transferable property. Not a person.' "

Jaffe doesn't hesitate. "Your Honors, the prosecutor is partially right. At the heart of this case are the words *person, people*. Are clones people? Lets me direct this to my co-counsel, Mr. John Quincy Adams."

The biograph is dressed in period clothing, which makes him seem very real. I know how important his argument is going to be, so I have my fingers crossed.

"Your Honors and friends of the court, this is a case I will hold as dear to my heart as I have the *Amistad* case. In the *Amistad* case that I argued before the US Supreme Court, nobody liked the idea of slaves rebelling against the captain and choosing to be free. The *Amistad* slaves had to go to court to win their freedom back that had been wrongfully taken in the first place. And here we are again arguing the same type of case."

"Mr. Jaffe," Justice Nagishana says, "I don't like being lectured to by a computer. I will let the biograph continue out of deference to who he was in real life. We are all familiar with the *Amistad* case and the role the former president played in the Africans' defense. But let's keep his comments pertinent to this case, at this time."

"What is a human being?" Adams begins in a less strident tone. "According to scholarship that dates back to ancient Greece, we find that mankind has been asking that same question. And of course they have come up with many different answers. In summary, the *essentia*, Latin for *essence*, is that by which a thing is what it is; the intrinsic nature of it. Early church documents state that the *essentia* of man consists in his being a rational creature of the universe. Physical details cannot change the *essentia*. Color of skin, length of hair, height, weight, education, strength, mastery of weapons, and others, are attributes that can't change the essence. Just because a clone has a fake hand or a clone has orange skin, does it change their essence?"

Mr. Adams gives a bow and sits down.

"Is he implying the cyborg laws are unjust?" the justice from Russia asks Jaffe.

"Yes."

This man Jaffe is good! I wish I could yell out loud something encouraging. A good swifting shout would go over like two dead flies, but it's what I want to do! Yeah!

I'm called to be a witness. The questioning begins.

"Carlos, did you copy and make available to everyone, even the justices, the memories of you, Houston, and Leanna over the last year or so?" Mr. Jaffe asks me while looking at the justices. Mom nudges me. I quickly compose myself.

"Yes," I say nervously. I look over at the light to make sure it shows green.

"Did you experience the memories of Leanna's time at the Topas Corporation when they were reprogramming her?" Jaffe asks me.

"Yes," I say a little more confidently. Mom squeezes my hand, letting me know I am doing fine.

"Are the clones people who have been changed into programmed creatures?"

Thomas interrupts. "I object. The boy is not an expert on this level. He can't answer this question. But we have someone who can. Dr. Marcus Pace."

No containing me. "Dad!" I shout.

"Marcus!" Mom shouts over me.

He turns toward our voices. Then drops his head as he proceeds to Mr. Thomas's table.

Bang!

Bang!

Bang!

"Order in this court!" Supreme Court Justice Nagishana snaps.

"Please, Dad, don't undercut us," I whisper too softly to hear, hoping I can teleport my thoughts to him.

"Is a clone a human being?" Mr. Thomas asks.

I'm holding my breath . . . waiting.

"Yes."

Exhale . . .

The courtroom erupts into cheers and jeers. The gavel slams long and hard, but people are jumping around like they're at a celebration. Mom is crying. I think I am, too. Dad is the first person of his status to speak in favor of the clones and cyborgs. And I know how far he has come and what he must have gone through to get to this point in his thinking.

Finally, we come back to order. Chief Justice Nagishana is very stern and emphatic. "Another outbreak like that and we will clear the court. Please continue, Dr. Pace."

"If you listened to Mr. Adams, you heard him say the essence of a person is his being a rational creature. Another way of putting it is, to be sentient — to be self-aware. Before meeting Dr. Ayala, I was convinced that clones were not human. It may still take time for me to accept these new ideas. Leanna Deberry is a healthy and smart girl with a great future ahead of her."

Jaffe asks Dr. Pace, "A belief is hard to change. How did Dr. Ayala help enlighten you about clones?"

Dad looks at Dr. Ayala. I see the venerable doctor nod ever so slightly, as if giving Dad permission. Dad swallows hard. I'm wondering what it is my father is getting ready to say. "He told me he was a clone."

What! Every eye turns toward the green light. *Ping!* It flashes green.

The room is tingling with low-level twitter. It's intense yet still, just the way it is before a thunderstorm. People want to talk, but they dare not, for fear of being put out. Nobody wants to miss what's coming next, especially me.

Dad explains that the original Ayala was a student of Dr. Montgomery. Ayala and five other assistants cloned themselves to test the stabilizer.

"The other five are here today." He points to three men and two women who are close in age to Dr. Ayala. They stand up. Impressive! They're prominent people from all over the world — an award-winning actress, a university president, an accomplished violinist, a bestselling author, and a world-recognized architect. I am surprised and so are the other people in the room.

Dad continues. "These men and women have had long, productive lives, proving that the stabilizer works. With this evidence, plus Leanna, it wasn't difficult for me to be convinced that unaltered clones are sentient beings capable of being productive citizens."

Dad comes to sit by us. We all three hug. I love my father after all.

"I have one more witness before we rest our case," says Jaffe. To my surprise, he accepts White Light from Dad. Jaffe asks permission to place White Light on the table in front of the justices. He is granted permission.

"How'd you get her to come?" I ask Dad.

"She really wants to find a peaceful solution. It was her idea."

The justices examine White Light. So do Mitch Thomas and his team.

Silence.

Jaffe places White Light on his table. He turns on his comm-pad to translator mode. "White Light, will you say a few words to make sure the translator is working?"

"I am White Light. Not a rock. I am leader of the Crystalline colony located on Mars. In our culture, it is a basic principle of law: Each person has a right to speak directly to those who have harmed them. That is why I am here." Green light flashes. White Light flashes two yellows, a green, and a long, bright light. The truth monitor holds steady on green. White Light sighs. "Poor thing. A one lighter. Where did you find that Crystalline?"

In spite of themselves, the justices smile. Several chuckle softly. They are way too dignified to laugh.

"Have we harmed you?" Justice Granbury, of the United States, asks, bringing it back to the serious tone.

"Yes. Why do you have to be human to be free?" White Light asks him. "Dr. Marcus Pace tried to force Crystallines to power your new spaceships."

"Okay. You're telling us the power crystals are alive?" Justice Granbury asks, looking at Dad, who nods his agreement.

"We are under the protection of The O," says White Light.

"Wait," the chief justice commands. "I want to see The O. Are they even real?"

"As you wish." Three cloaked figures materialize in the courtroom. We can't see their faces or hands.

Justice Granbury leaps to his feet. "Who are you?"

"What is this — some magician's trick? How dare you invade this session with foolishness?" says the chief justice. "I have never seen anything like what has happened here today. Who are you?"

"We are The O, and you called us into this session of your own free will."

"The O! Criminals! Enough is enough," the justice from Argentina says, standing up. "Dr. Pace, you are a traitor, unworthy of your high standing as a Federation scientist. These bio-things are a danger to our way of life, and now these masked and robed creatures are making a mockery of this hall of Justice. Spiller, I order you to clean this courtroom of clones by action that is permanent!"

Joe Spiller grins. "With pleasure," he whispers under his breath.

What? We can't believe what we've heard. A justice has ordered the deaths of all the clones in here. Everybody seems frozen in disbelief.

Chief Justice Nagishana pounds her gavel and tries to rescind the order. Meanwhile, Spiller launches his biobot at Dr. Ayala. The thing's claws are extended, ready to tear Doc Doc to pieces.

Toby and Houston try to reach the doctor, but it's too late. Dad has stepped in front of Doc Doc, and the biobot digs its claws into Dad's chest. I scream as he falls, crashing hard on the floor. Lying on his back, Dad gasps for air between waves of pain. I'm completely stunned.

The justices are being escorted out of the room and into safety. I tell Mom to hide under the table with the others. I hear Mom's protests, but I've got to go see about Dad. I've never been so scared in my life, until I hear Houston saying, "Look out!" Apache springs to life out of Houston.

A silver, spinning blade whizzes by my face, barely missing me. I instinctively turn, knowing exactly where the blade is headed. Spiller's military training makes him the perfect killing machine. Apache knocks Leanna to the floor. The spinning knife barely misses Leanna.

I finally reach Dad. He's not going to make it.

MEMORY STICK
SECTOR QE-3
NOWHERE

I don't remember how I got here or even where here is. But it is no place that I remember.

I'm standing on something solid. It's not rock or ground. I can't see what it is. All I can see is me. I see my hands, my clothes, but nothing else. I finally notice Justice Granbury standing next to me. I can see him, but I can't see anything around him. This place is bizarre!

"Is that you, sir?" I say, touching him to make sure he is real.

"Yes, Carlos. It's me. Who else is here?"

"Sir, Justice, sir," I say, being polite, "I'm not sure what's going on. But I'm worried about my father. He might be dead."

"No, son. I'm okay," Dad says, appearing in front of me. I touch him, too, looking for signs of wounds. Nothing. He really is okay.

"It's The O, Carlos," White Light says to me, flashing colors in Dad's hand. "Nowhere is where we are," she says. Even her bright flashing light can't give this "place" any definition. We're just here. "Nowhere is a place where time doesn't exist."

"Spoken like a true gemaginist," says Justice Granbury.

"The correct question, Carlos, is not *where are we*? But *why are we here?* I think I understand," he says, looking at White Light closer.

Sensing they are there, I call out, "Okay, O, tell us why we are here."

Out of the darkness, the cloaked images appear. The O. White Light speaks to them in colors. White Light responds so we all can hear and understand. "Yes, humans are self-important. If it is not about them, then it is not important."

"Not all of us," Justice Granbury says.

"In court, White Light asked you a simple question. Why do you have to be human to be free?" The O says.

"Oh, I got that," says Justice Granbury. "You want us to learn from our past so that we don't turn Crystallines into slaves in the future. Does that summarize what you are trying to tell us humans?"

"Yes, that has always been our goal," says The O, and they disappear.

A big gust of wind blows me over. And that's all I remember.

MEMORY STICK
SECTOR QE-2B
REPEAT

I get what Mom is saying. I haven't thought about the whole world watching. A big gust of wind almost throws us off balance. Mom gives my black, unruly hair a brush with her hand, and we enter the Peace Palace.

The O have reset time. Everything is as it was before—almost. "All rise. The court now sits," says the court clerk.

The room instantly becomes quiet. Fifteen justices wearing black robes walk into the room from a side door leading to their seats at the front of the room. Justice Granbury is the last justice to enter the room.

Déjà vu?

In unison, the justices stand, raise their right hands, and begin speaking in Latin:

"Constans et perpetua voluntas, jus suum cuique tribuendi."

"What did they say?" Mom asks me.

"They said, 'The constant and perpetual will to secure to everyone his own right.' I think it's the slogan of the court."

The justices continue their oath in English. "I solemnly declare that I will perform my duties and exercise my powers as judge honorably, faithfully, impartially, and of good conscience." They sit down. Not everything is exactly the same, we didn't hear Latin before.

"My mom didn't lie to me." The light flashes red. "I mean she is my mother. I believed I was a First." The light flashes green. Leanna looks at me. I give her the thumbs-up sign.

Then it's getting close to the crazy part. . . .

"Okay. You're telling us the power crystals are alive?" Justice Granbury asks, looking at Dad, who nods his agreement.

"We are under the protection of The O," says White Light.

"Wait," the chief justice commands. "I want to see The O. Are they even real?"

"As you wish." Three cloaked figures materialize in the courtroom. We can't see their faces or hands.

"Houston," I whisper, "you and Toby get ready. There's going to be a rumble."

Justice Granbury leaps to his feet. "Who are you?"

"What is this — some magician's trick? How dare you invade this session with foolishness?" says the chief justice. "I have never seen anything like what has happened here today. Who are you?"

"We are The O, and you called us into this session of your own free will."

"Enough is enough," the justice from Argentina says, standing up. "We've been invaded by aliens. We need protection."

Joe Spiller grins. "You've got it," he whispers underneath his breath.

Spiller throws his biobot at The O. They vanish. So the

biobot chooses Doc Doc. But Houston's Apache jumps from his shoulder. The wolf snatches the biobot in midair and rips it apart.

Bang!

Bang!

Bang!

Chief Justice Nagishana hits the gavel. "Guards, please remove Joe Spiller from this courtroom."

"I didn't mean for him to attack anybody," the Argentinian justice says.

"We know." Then moving on, the chief justice adds, "We are ready to make our decision." When the room is totally silent, the chief justice speaks.

"I believe the new evidence has decided the case for us. Does anyone disagree?" she says, looking at the rest of the justices.

All the justices shake their heads one at a time. "Granbury, can you simply state the position of the court?" the chief justice asks him. I'm amazed that all of the justices seem to agree without discussing it.

"The law of our world states that slavery is illegal. The Thirteenth Amendment to the US Constitution forbids slavery. This has not changed for centuries. Slavery is illegal for any person or sentient being inherently capable of free choice," he says, looking at White Light, who is sitting beside him at the table.

"This is a new life-form. It is a Crystalline, obviously not human, but sentient none the less. They live in communities that are governed by laws, and they ask only to be left alone to live as they choose — in freedom."

I look around the room and people are crying for joy. Others are crying because they see their way of life threatened, their belief systems under attack. Leanna and her mother are embracing. My own mother is hugging me. We know the long, hard struggle so many people have been through to get to this place . . . including The O's.

"If we agree to extend freedom to Crystallines, who aren't human, how can we deny the rights of clones and cyborgs who have also proven to be sentient?" Granbury continues. "We must judge them all based on their *essentia* and not their attributes. Therefore we agree unanimously that the clone codes and cyborg laws are fundamentally illegal and are void. The Topas Corporation shall stop all cloning until there can be a full investigation into their cloning policies and practices.

"In summary: All persons and sentient beings have equal rights under existing law. No new law shall be created or existing laws revised that infringe upon the civil rights, freedom, justice, and equality of any sentient beings. So says this court."

Bang!

Bang!

Bang!

Chief Justice Nagishana dismisses the court. The justices exit. What a way to end!

We all race to get outside where we can cheer and shout for joy!

MEMORY STICK
SECTOR QE-4
CELEBRATE

August 9, 2171

One day we will celebrate this as a worldwide holiday — a time to remember when, to paraphrase another great moment, *we made one small step for a human, one giant leap for humankind.* WOW!

The celebrations went on for weeks. Leanna and Houston and Rizin laughed and talked about every detail of the court hearings. We had won a major victory for our causes and we felt victorious. Even RUBy and White Light got into the party spirit and put on a light show that was spangling.

White Light is staying here a while to talk about the role of Crystallines in the space program. RUBy and I are thrilled. Leanna's going back to school. Houston is off to Georgia Tech. And Rizin is back on the Moon. No war or threats of any looming.

It feels good being with all my neighbors and friends. But most of all, it feels great to be home with Mom and Dad. I'm working with Dad and it seems right now. We are a family but my family has grown to include a lot of unlikely beings.

THE END . . .

AND THE BEGINNING

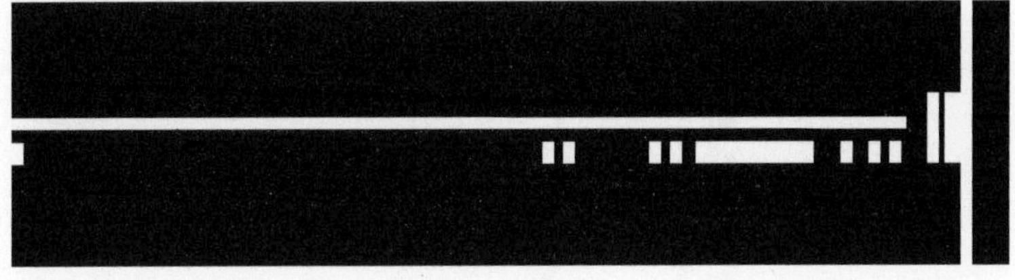

THE YEAR IS 2172

In the main office of The WFN, The O visit the presidents of several nations. The O compliment humanity for the changes they have made regarding freedom and justice. "There's still a lot of work needed. We are especially pleased with the decision of The World Supreme Court. There are plans being made to match human children with Crystallines in preschool. So they grow together as partners."

Though close, The O still do not feel humanity is ready to come into deep space.

The leaders plead their case. But The O tell them that they will be welcomed into their worlds when the time is right for all those concerned. "You have several more hurdles to clear," say The O. "We will be very interested in how you handle the mutants. . . ."

"What mutants? Who? Where?"

The O respond, "We have said too much. We must go. But we will be watching."

The leaders push to know. "When will we be ready?"

The answer comes quickly. "When you no longer need to be watched."

ABOUT THE AUTHORS

Newbery Honor winner Patricia C. McKissack has collaborated on many critically acclaimed books with her husband, Fredrick L. McKissack. Together, they are the authors of numerous award winners, including *Rebels Against Slavery: American Slave Revolts* and *Black Hands, White Sails: The Story of African-American Whalers*, both Coretta Scott King Honor Books, and *Sojourner Truth: Ain't I a Woman?* a Coretta Scott King Honor Book and winner of the Boston Globe/Horn Book Award. Patricia and Fredrick McKissack live in St. Louis, Missouri.

John McKissack, the son of Patricia and Fredrick, is a licensed mechanical engineer. *The Clone Codes* marks his debut as a writer. John is married to Michelle McKissack, and they are the parents of three sons, Peter, James Everett, and John. They reside in Memphis, Tennessee.

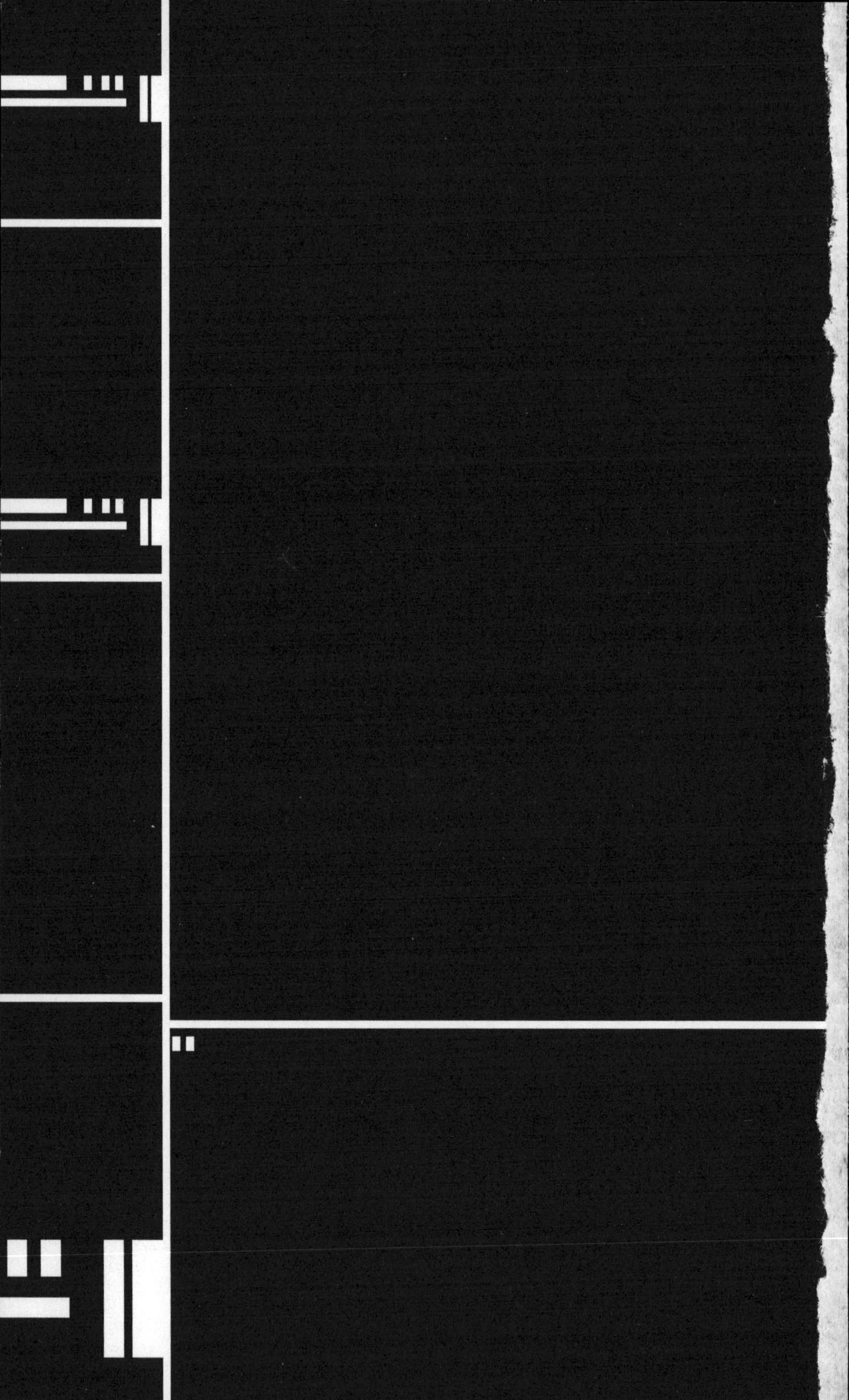